happy hour

and

other sorrows

J.T. TWISSEL

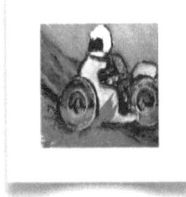

Cover Art by Unknown Cartoonist for The Overseas
Edited by Duke Miller

This is a work of fiction. Names, characters, places, brands, media, and incidents are either the product of the author's imagination or are used fictitiously. Any resemblance to similarly named places or to persons living or deceased is unintentional.

Print ISBN 978-0-9979426-6-8

Contents

CHAPTER 1

AMERIKANERS

"WHAT TROUBLES YOU?" Asked a certain Frau Schwimmer in a voice quivering on irritation. All of the other passengers were nesting comfortably in their seats, trying to catch a few hours of sleep before landing on the other side of the world. But not the young woman assigned to the aisle seat next to her.

"Nichts. Nothing," The young woman replied, but ... thirty thousand feet below lay snow and ice infinitum. Whiteness upon whiteness upon whiteness. Ahead, the veil of darkness called night. Soon the plane would cut through that veil like a silver arrow rounding the curve of the earth, that is if it didn't crash land in the frozen wastelands of Northern Canada. If that happened, Flight 32 would be lost forever. No search and rescue team would ever be able find the wreckage in all that whiteness. The passengers would have to eat each other to stay alive, like the Donner party. That is, if the plane landed intact, which it wouldn't. It would tumble across the tundra, leaving bodies mangled in the metal, eventually found and devoured by hungry polar bears.

The fidgeting continued. Frau Schwimmer noted the crumpled map on the young woman's lap. "Wo gehen sie?

"I don't know. The town is called Gunthersblum but I

can't find it on the map."

"We will find!" Frau Schwimmer pulled an industrial sized map of Germany out of her woven travel bag and patted the young woman on the hand. "Have not angst."

Easy for her to say. She knows where she's going!

The plane shook violently. The seat belt lights flashed. "Air turbulence," the pilot announced in English, then German, then French.

He's lying. The plane's lost an engine, sucked in a goose, or ruptured a gas line. It was going down.

Frau Schwimmer unfolded her map and calmly spread it out over their two tray tables. "Ist Gunthersblum Nord or Sud?"

"I don't know." *I know what she's thinking. Who flies to the other side of the world without knowing precisely where they're going?.*

"First we check index." Frau Schwimmer ran her finger down the list of towns and villages: "Gunthersblum. Nein, Gunthersberg? Nein. Guntherslauten? Nein." She turned to the hapless young woman."You have perhaps written down the wrong name. There is no Gunthersblum in Deutschland!"

* * *

When her mother had called two weeks earlier citing a need to talk *PDQ*, (one of her favorite words, along with *crap* and its cousin, *holy crap*) the young woman now getting on Frau Schwimmer's last nerve naturally assumed the worst. Her mother was dying. It was all of that smoking and drinking and lying in the sun until she was the color of week-old hamburger. It was her diet of Twinkies and chicken pot pies, Tater Tots, canned spaghetti, and pot roast full of grizzle. All Mother's bad habits had finally caught up with her.

She'd raced home as quickly as she could on her Honda 90 (max speed 35 mph) through the smoke from a wildfire just south of Reno. Ashes covered the cars like radioactive snow. Ashes covered her helmet and made her hair white. Ashes greyed the sky. Someday they won't be able to stop the fires, she thought, and the whole damn valley will burn to ashes. Someday..

Her mother stood in the kitchen ironing a pile of men's boxers. It was a hundred degrees outside and she was ironing. She barely looked up when her daughter ran breathlessly into the house. "Shut the damn door!" she said as she took another drag on her Camel. "Don't let any of that smoke in the house."

Without any of the appropriate 'how are you doings' she waved an envelope in the young woman's face. "It's a letter from my brother. Read it. He wants to give you a graduation present. "

"That's it? I graduated from high school two years ago. I thought you were dying."

"Dying? Holy crap, what an imagination you have! It's a wonder you ever get any sleep."

The young woman took the envelope from her mother's hands. "This letter's from Germany. What's Uncle Dan doing in Europe"

"For crying out loud! It's not from Dan! Dan'll never leave Rhode Island! It's from your other uncle."

3

"Uncle Bob? Oh my God. He's still alive?"

* * *

Once Frau Schwimmer determined that the young woman had indeed gotten herself in fit of angst for no good reason, that it was simply a mistake and nothing more, the logical thing for both of them to do was to try to get some rest. She put her map away and shut off the overhead light; she donned her sleep mask and turned toward the window. She concluded by pulling down the shade with a pronounced snap.

The young woman sighed. In her hurry to get a passport and all the necessary shots to travel to Europe, she hadn't had time to verify her uncle's location on a map. She thought of pulling her backpack down from the overhead bin and showing Frau Schwimmer the letter she'd received but instead she shut off her overhead light. She'd irritated the good frau enough.

Sleep was impossible. If only, if only, she kept thinking, she'd been given some time to plan but she'd been pressured by her mother whose adoration of her brilliant younger brother's cosmopolitan and glamorous lifestyle was rivaled only by her adoration of her only son. The young woman *must* seize *immediately* upon this undeserved opportunity before her uncle came to his senses and rescinded his offer! There was no time for questioning or investigation! It wasn't as if the young woman's other forays into life had been successful! Fail, fail, fail—

fail—that's all she'd ever done.

For hours the young woman sat in the dark and listened to the engines struggle, the metal platters rattle in the galley and the stewardesses whisper…the engines struggle, the metal platters rattle, in the gallery and the stewardesses whisper until she was certain they'd flown into the Twilight Zone and that the cycle would never end.

The nightmare ended when the pilot announced that he'd spotted the coast of Ireland. The shades lifted one by one. Stewardesses passed out coffee first and then orange juice and croissants. People rose and stretched and then formed long lines at the bathrooms with washcloths and toothbrushes in hand. The pilot reported the weather and local time in Frankfurt and began providing instructions for customs forms in German, French and English.

A few hours later the plane began its descent over the green hills surrounding Frankfurt.

Frau Schwimmer noted that the young woman's mood seemed to have lightened significantly. It had to be the sunlight. It's hard to be anxious when the sun is shining. She insisted on them exchanging seats so that the young woman could look out the window.

"It's so green!"

"Naturlich."

"Where I come from it's always brown by this time of year."

Frau Schwimmer had her own opinions about the

area around Frankfurt. Probably because she and her husband were lucky enough to live on the outskirts of Oberammergau. They could see the Alps from their back deck! No doubt the uncle this young American claimed to be visiting was with the US Army. Military personnel were all over that area. Not just the Americans. The British, the Australians and even the French. The war had been over for twenty five years and Germany was *still* an occupied country.

As the plane disembarked, the young woman turned to Frau Schwimmer with a smile: "I'll be okay. Really. I don't know why I was so panicked. I guess it's just my first trip to Europe."

But the older woman was unconvinced and refused to leave her side as they waited for their luggage and maneuvered through customs. Once in the reception area, Frau Schwimmer's husband, a trim man dressed in tweed similar to hers, was front and center. After a perfunctory peck on the cheek, she explained the situation to him. They were going to keep this poor young woman company until her uncle arrived.

"Ach du lieber," he mumbled.

"What looks like your uncle?" Frau Schwimmer asked as they settled on hard plastic chairs.

It had been at least ten years since the young woman had seen her uncle but she remembered him well. He was tall and stern, like the big Swedes on her mother's side of the family, and dressed exactly as one would expect a government man, in a charcoal-grey suit, white shirt and thin striped tie. Sweat rolled down his face as the temperature on that summer day in Washington DC hovered near ninety with, what felt like, 100 percent humidity. He wore his sandy hair in a crew cut and his eyes were hidden behind thick, black-rimmed glasses.

"He's a big man," She finally said, "Mit monokel."

"Ein grosse mann. Mit monokel?" Frau Schwimmer asked, pointing to the eyeglasses her husband wore.

"Yeah. Uber ein grosse mann."

"Ein grosse man," Frau Schwimmer said, scanning the room.

The first group of arrivals were soon absorbed into the waiting crowds, embraced and then hustled out the exits. They were soon followed by a second group, also greeted, embraced and hustled out the exits and then a third.

Every time another group of travelers came and went, Herr Schwimmer glanced at his wristwatch and every time he glanced at his wristwatch the young woman pleaded with the couple: "Please leave. Please go home. I have a return ticket."

Herr Schwimmer'd finally had enough and was on his feet ready to go when his wife pointed to the man foraging through the crowds toward them. "Ach! Ein gross man mit monokel! He wore a Hawaiian shirt, loosely buttoned over his belly, khaki shorts, and a pair of thick leather sandals, no socks.

"My god!" The young woman gasped. The crewcut uncle she remembered now sported a sun-bleached Beatle haircut.

"Riley Anne? Is that you?" The man asked scanning

the young woman's face for some sign of that child he hadn't seen for years. Did she look like her mother? Did she match the general description sent? Was she the right age, size? His mind was pulling all known facts about his niece from a cerebral database.

"Hello, Uncle Bob."

"Hurry up. We're double-parked!" The uncle said, grabbing the young woman's arm.

She picked up her duffel and turned to thank the Schwimmers. "Danke—"

"Did I mention we're double parked! I don't suppose you could have been waiting outside on the damned curb like a normal person!"

The Schwimmers watched as the grosser man mit monokel dragged his niece out the exit. They watched as he shoved her into the back seat of a beat up Volkswagen bug parked halfway up on the curb and climbed into the passenger seat. They watched as the little car slipped off the curb, wobbled like a drunken sailor and then butted its way into the traffic stream. And then they turned to each other and said in unison: "Ach du liber! Amerikaners!"

CHAPTER 2

DEATH ON THE AUTOBAHN

"GILBERTO, meet my lovely niece. Now ... hit it!

The man behind the wheel of the Volkswagen glanced into the rear view mirror, first with a smile to the "lovely niece" and then beyond her to what had spooked her uncle. "I see him!"

"Then hit it!"

What both men had seen was a traffic cop in an olive green uniform waving his baton and shouting as he tried to catch up with them.

"He wants us to stop, Uncle Bob!" The young woman said.

"Go!" Shouted her uncle.

The driver swerved further into the traffic stream igniting a firestorm of horns and causing the traffic cop to retreat to the safety of the curb.

"That was close." The uncle turned to his niece and chuckled. "Look at your face. You'd think we just committed murder. They're not going to chase after us just to give us a parking ticket. Speaking of which, did you remember to get your international driver's license, Riley Anne?"

"Yes, Uncle Bob, of course I did. You asked me to and I did. But I hate to be called Riley Anne. Do you suppose you could just call me Riley?"

"Okey dokey. You know you won't be able to drive over here if you didn't get it."

"Sheesh, Uncle Bob, I got the license like you asked. What's the big deal?"

"Your uncle lost his license a while back." The driver explained, winking at the young woman in the rearview mirror, "And my name is Gil not Gilberto."

Somehow the fact that her uncle had lost his license wasn't a big shock. "So were you speeding or something, Uncle Bob?"

"*Or something* sounds good."

"The German police like to pull DACs over on trumped-up charges and suspend their licenses. It's called harassing the occupiers. That's what happened to your uncle."

"*Right.*"

Gil laughed. "Well, maybe that's not exactly what happened to your uncle."

They were on the outskirts of the Frankfurt, passing modern structures with few architectural flourishes. The roads were smooth, the sidewalks clean, the gardens well kept but not ornamental. It wasn't how the young woman had imagined Europe, an endless, gray suburb.

"What's a dac?" Riley asked.

"Dac?"

"Yeah you said you and Uncle Bob were dacs."

"Oh yeah, it stands for Department of Army Civilian. Your uncle and I work for the Army."

"You do? I thought you worked for the CIA, Uncle

Bob, and decoded secret messages."

There was a pause and then the young woman's uncle began to chuckle. "The CIA? Cripes, is that what your mother told you?"

"Yup. The story I heard was they dragged you away from college the night you graduated and ever since you've been working for them. That's why we hardly ever hear from you. And that's why every year those men in dark suits came to our neighborhood, asking everyone if we were hanging out with communists."

"Routine background checks. That's all they were. Not to burst your bubble about your old Unc, but the truth (which has always been a little bit hard for my sister to grasp) is that I work for the budget department. My *job* is to tell the generals when they're spending too much money."

Riley caught her uncle's curious glance in the rear view mirror. He had the same unnerving pale blue eyes as her mother with just a pinprick of black in the center to prove he was human.

"That must make you popular with the generals."

"Heh. A smart ass like your ma. Then I guess you've figured out why I invited you over."

"You need a driver?"

"Just until your auntie gets back from Greece. Then you can take the car and go wherever you want..." Something on the side of the road distracted him and he began jerking in his seat as if he could direct the car via muscle spasms.

"Damn it Gilberto! You're going to miss the autobahn!

Quit making goo-goo eyes at my niece and keep your eyes on the road."

"Calm down. I see it," Gil swerved hard to the right, and began accelerating down a ramp that grew narrower and narrower as its block walls grew higher and higher. She could hear the of roar of engines echoing against the concrete walls like hungry beasts.

"Hang on to whatever you can, Riley. This is the autobahn," Gil said. "Germany's answer to the Indy 500. There is no speed limit, no rules except to get out of the way and then ... no place *to* get out of the way."

They flew onto the autobahn landing with a bounce behind two battered delivery trucks. In the other three lanes, high-speed vehicles rocketed past them with their horns ablaze.

"Move over before we get stuck behind these old clunkers!" Uncle Bob ordered.

"In case you haven't noticed, Bob, we are in an old clunker."

"Come on, come on. This old baby can handle it."

"I don't think so."

"Hell, I've gotten her up to eighty!"

"Ha!"

"Hit the gas. You'll see..."

Gil rolled his eyes and then veered into the next lane. At his gentle urging the Volkswagen briefly sprung to action and then, feeling her age and no doubt abuse, whimpered and begged to be put out of her misery. Within seconds a black BMW was perched on the rear bumper, lights flashing, horn blaring, the angry driver pounding his fist in the air. He hated them! Hated their vile presence in his lane and in his country and now it was his time for revenge.

"Pull over!" Riley cried. "Please ..."

"Hit the gas!" Her uncle ordered.

"What do you think I was doing?"

"You couldn't even get past that old clunker. Why, if I was driving..." .

"Yeah, yeah, Uncle Bob. Like you could race a Ferrari in this old heap!"

"I could, Niecey, I could! When I'm behind the wheel this old baby really flies."

Riley shrank down as far as she could in the back seat and closed her eyes. Her first day in Europe would also be last on earth. What a waste! Dying before she'd seen anything other than the Frankfurt airport and the autobahn, her body parts indistinguishable from the metal of a dozen cars when the inevitable pileup occurred. She wondered if her friends on the other side of the world could sense her imminent death as they slept. "Last night I dreamt of Riley and now I hear that she is gone. Killed on the autobahn, her first day in Europe. What a waste."

As she contemplated the effect news of her death might have on her friends and family, she felt the car veer to the right and begin to rise from the pit.

Ah, this is the real Europe, she thought as they emerged to a different world entirely, to cobblestone streets and cottages with thatched roofs, to twisty roads that ran past farms, over gentle hills, and along streams.

The real Europe. The one she'd always dreamt about. A different world from the surreal deserts dotted with gaudy casinos and strip malls that she'd come from. This green landscape seemed so clean, so pure. The land of peaceful, loving peasants, charming villages with helpful shopkeepers and—

"Gilberto, did you get a look at the knockers on Lou's new secretary?"

"Molly, you mean Molly, right?"

"Yeah, I guess that's her name. You know, the big ones are fun to cuddle but there is something to be said for frisky little titties. The French have a saying that the perfect size tit fits into a champagne glass. What do you think of that Gilberto? You like the frisky little titties?"

"Ah, Uncle Bob. I'm in the back seat."

"So? You got a thing against tits?"

"I can't believe I actually thought you were a spy."

"Spies don't like tits?"

He continued on with his admiration of tits until finally, as the sun lay low in the sky, Gil announced they'd reached the illusive town of Gunthersblum. Frau Schwimmer had been wrong. It did exist, not as Riley had imagined, an alpine village surrounded by fields of flowers. It was a crook in the road in a green through drab landscape. It was Eureka, Nevada, only greener. There were no stoplights, sidewalks, or street lights. In fact, it was devoid of people as they drove through. Most of the villagers lived on the outskirts of town, her uncle explained, and worked in the surrounding sugar beet fields, their day beginning long before dawn with a good shot of schnapps to ward off the cold. The town center, he further explained, contained a "grocery store slash pharmacy slash gift shop," and a "bar slash roadhouse slash diner." All were dark.

"If you're looking for excitement, this isn't going to be the place for you. Most of the villagers go to sleep with the sun."

"Right now I just wanna go to bed!"

They drove up the hill to a row of modern, two-story stucco houses, each with a small front yard, driveway, and iron fence. Her uncle's house, only recognizable as the third from the corner, was dark.

Gil carried Riley's duffel bag into the foyer while her uncle disappeared into a dimly lit kitchen. After *his* ordeal, he said, he needed a Scotch. "Join me," he said to Gil but the younger man declined, citing a need to get back to town.

"Where are the bedrooms? I need to crash."

"Upstairs. What an ordeal this day has been. My niece is not even smart enough to wait on the curb to be picked up. What have I gotten myself into?" Uncle Bob said, pouring himself a drink.

While she recognized in her uncle the family's warped sense of humor, she wondered, as she walked up the stairs and into the dark: *What have I gotten myself into?*

CHAPTER 3

THE PUTZIE

THE NEXT MORNING the young woman awoke in a puddle of sunlight certain the day before had been a dream: the endless flight, the German couple who'd kept her company while she'd waited, the machismo zoom pit called the autobahn, and the young man whose touch still made her tingle. Although…That part of the dream, that part of the dream had to have been the side effect of too little sleep and a boatload of anxiety. Absolutely. Positively. She had a boyfriend. In fact, he was the one who'd urged her to take time off from school to have that one last adventure before they, in his words, got serious. A boyfriend who was admired by all her friends and family and who was considered an excellent catch.

No, she had not come to Europe for romance but to see a bit of the world before getting serious. She was after all, twenty years old. Time to get serious, whatever the hell that meant. But, after this break.

She sat up, rubbed the gunk from her eyes and smelt her armpits. "Oh my God. Do I stink!" Then she looked around the room. Other than a pine wardrobe sitting all alone in the corner, the twin sized bed she'd face-planted on the night before was the only piece of furniture in the room. The one unscreened window had been thrown wide open exposing the view. The day before had been no dream. What she saw out the window was definitely not downtown Reno Nevada.

The first order of business was to find a bathroom. She was pre-menstrual, starving, and had a headache the size of Rhode Island. What a horrible way to start my first day in Europe, she though. A nice hot bath, that's what I need. Then clean clothes and then, food.

She found a bathroom at the top of a staircase leading to the downstairs. The floors were cold to her bare feet and the uncovered window made her feel on display as she peed. And it housed not one but two toilets. One of them looked like an ordinary American toilet but the other had a ledge. Strange, she thought as she filled the tub. Why do they need two toilets? One for number one and the other for number two? There had been no mention of the two toilet situation in either the French or German classes she'd taken. But there they were. Two friggin' toilets.

As she soaked she began to imagine the day's adventures. Perhaps her uncle planned to show her the countryside. If not (which seemed more likely) she could wander down to the village to window shop, try the local delicacies, and buy postcards to send home. She imagined happy, smiling villagers, all eager to help her explore their ancient town and learn its history. Maybe she'd find someone her age, someone who'd become a lifelong friend and pen pal.

In the midst of her musings the door flew open, and woman of around thirty marched in wearing a starched white apron at least two sizes too big for her. "Slaftz du yest?" She asked as she pulled laundry from a nearby wicker hamper.

"Pardon?"

"Slaftz, slaftz!"

"Ich komme aus America. Ich bin..."

"Nein, du slaftz zu weil!" The woman repeated, grabbing all the towels. "Muss saubermachen!"she said, stomping out of the room.

"Wait! I need a towel!" Riley said to which the woman scoffed as she disappeared.

That must have been Uncle Bob's cleaning lady, Riley thought as she rose from the tub and, having no other choice, covered herself with her dirty clothes and ran back to the bedroom. While she'd been in the tub some-one had stripped the bed, flung the blankets over the window ledge, and emptied her duffel bag, stashing her clothes neatly in the wardrobe. Her family had never had a maid or even a cleaning woman and so she felt...violat-ed. Someone had seen her cheap underwear and faded blue jeans. Not to mention her thick leather Birkenstocks. What must she have thought?

The house was much larger than she suspected. Be-sides the bathroom, there were four blah bedrooms up-stairs, each containing a bed with a nightstand and a wardrobe but few paintings, pictures, or knick-knacks. It was as if no one really lived there. The first floor was domi-nated by a good-sized kitchen, in the corner of which stood the cleaning lady, stuffing clothes and linen into the washing machine. The kitchen also had a farmer's table with several sturdy wooden chairs and a view of the street in front. The living room also faced the street. The only thing in the living room that did not scream "army issue" was the pile of books on the coffee table.

"Pardon,"she said to the cleaning lady, after the searching the house and finding no trace of her uncle. "Bitte. Wo ist mein Oncle?"

"Herr Neilson ist arbeiten. Work! Jetzt, Ich muss saubermachen."

Work, ah yes. That made sense. It was Friday morning.

The cleaning lady stayed for another hour, scoffing at her feeble attempts to have a conversation. When she returned to the States, Riley decided she would ask Herr Assmus why he made his students memorize the history of Koenig Ludwig's castle? It was hardly a good conversation starter with a normal German. *Excuse me, but did you know Koenig Ludwig built his famous castle in 1850?* Nor was "Where is the library?" Why would anyone want to go to the library in a country where they could barely speak, let alone *read*, in the native language? Of course, Herr Assmus would be shocked that one of his least promising German students could make such an insightful suggestion. *Ach, not you! The dumbkopf from third period!*

After the cleaning lady left Riley searched the cupboards in the kitchen for something to eat. To her surprise they were filled with such all American stables as Campbell's soup, Skippy peanut butter, Cheerios, Rice Krispies, Wonder Bread and instant mashed potatoes. No

German food. In fact, there was nothing more exotic than a few tins of Prince Albert sardines.

But she was hungry and so made a peanut butter sandwich and wandered out to the living room to take a look through the picture books. One of them, *The Rhine River Valley*, contained pictures of castles overlooking the river and charming rows of half-timber houses with flower pots in the windows, all under cloudless skies. Maybe that's where I am, she thought, the Rhine River valley. "Cool," she said aloud as she sat Indian-style on the stiff sofa and began leafing through the pages.

Two bites into her sandwich the phone in the hall rang.

CHAPTER 4

THE WHITE RABBIT

"YOU FINALLY GOT UP, did you?" It was her uncle. "That cleaning lady of yours…"

"You mean Putzie? Got you out of bed, did she?"

"Sort of."

"Ha! Well it's her day to clean and you were probably in her way. Ask her to show you where the train station is. If you can get down here by noon, I'll buy you lunch."

"The Putzie, as you call her, has left."

"Lazy, good-for-nothing girl! Okay. Walk down to the middle of the town. You can't possibly miss the train station."

"Where am I going?"

"Worms, of course. Shouldn't cost you more than a couple of marks."

"But I…"

"You don't have any money, right?"

"I just got here last night. I haven't had a chance to—"

"Cripes…Look in the drawer under the phone. There should be some spare change there."

A real German meal—bratwurst smothered in sauerkraut or—Wiener Schnitzel! She wrapped the peanut butter sandwich in plastic and was out the door in seconds.

Downtown Gunthersblum was little more than two block square of brick and stone buildings, none of which had any sort of business advertisement. None of which was a train station she couldn't possibly miss. Nor were the people out and about at that time of morning interested in helping a stranger to their village. One group of older women lugging vegetables and dragging toddlers behind them even hissed at the young American when she dared smile and wave to them.

"Pity's sake,"she said aloud, "I am not a child molester, ladies"

She heard a chuckle behind her and turned to see a lady with only a basket of onions to protect eyeing her with amusement from the shadowy eaves of a bus stop.

"Bitte. Wo ist die Bahnhof?" She asked the lady with the onions.

"Die Bahnhof?"

"Yeah. You know, trains, choo-choos?"

"Yah, yah," she laughed. "Choo-choos."She pointed across the road to a squat building whose sole sign read *Poste.*

"The post office is also the train station?"

"Yeah," the woman shrugged her shoulders."Naturlich."

Naturlich, of course, wasn't every post office also a train station? I'm getting played, she thought. She imagined the woman with the onions bragging to her family later that night: *Yeah, I told the American dummkopf the post office was also the train station and she believed me!*

But the woman with onions kept nodding her head

insistently. *Go. Go*

Okay. I'll go along with the joke, she thought as she crossed the road. I'll give you a story to tell your family.

Inside of the building was a sturdy wood table on which sat a scale and a rack containing pamphlets and forms. Along the walls were numbered mail slots and vending machines selling stamps and cigarettes. It *was* a post office. The two men huddled at the back of the room behind a cashier's booth looked up briefly as the young woman entered and then both went back to reading.

"Bahnhof?" She asked.

"Naturlich," The grayer of the two men snapped, pointing to a timetable posted against the back wall.

"Really?"

"Naturlich!"

She pondered the timetable for a few minutes before deciding that learning to read timetables in German was another thing sadly missing from Herr Assmus' syllabus.

"Ich gehe nach Worms," she said as sweetly as she could. She *was* the only customer in the Poste/Bahnhof which surely had to play in her favor.

But no.

"Vorms," the older man stiffly corrected her.

"Vorumms?"

"Vorms!".

She tried to explain. "Ich bin Americaner. Ich wohne mit mein Oncle Bob." *I'm an American; I'm living with my Uncle Bob.*

23

"Herr Nielson? Der grosser Americaner ist Oncle Boob?"

"Aber das name ist *Ba-ahhb*, not Boob."

"Heinrich," The older clerk said to his younger co-worker. "Der grosser Amerikaner ist ihre Oncle Boob!"

"Boob? Ha, ha, ha!"

Riley felt her cheeks burn. They were having such fun at her expense but at least they hadn't treated her like a malignant child molester. She gave up trying to correct them, bought her ticket, and went through the back door where—surprise, surprise—there were train tracks! The post office was the train station. Her faith in the goodness of the villagers was restored.

She took a position on the far side of the tracks to wait for the train as the postmen watched from the window. She waved and smiled. *Danke!* They responded with wild hand gestures. Then the one called Heinrich burst from the back door, ran over, and pulled her to the other side of the tracks. "Worms ist sud! Sud! Nicht nord!"

How was she supposed to know which way she was going? She was in a small town, waiting for a train to take her to a place she'd never even heard of: Worms, Germany. But she was grateful to the man when a few minutes later a steam train rumbled up to the station.

The conductor, a meticulously groomed man in a striped vest, crisp navy-blue suit and an engineer's cap, stepped down from one of the cars and motioned for the young woman to board. "Ich gehe nach Worms," She informed him to which he just grunted.

Once on board she took a seat by the window and

soon, for the first time in two days, felt at ease. Only a week earlier she'd been fighting with her mother in the Kmart over the price of shoes and now she was rolling past ancient villages with names like "Gubberstagamer" and "Leuseundorfer" and some even longer.

At each stop the conductor climbed off the train, oversaw the exit and entrance of passengers, looked at his pocket watch, and then announced the train's departure. Between each stop he marched down the aisles examining the tickets of the newly boarded, always with a suspicious eye towards the young American. A couple of times he even stopped and demanded to see her passport, as if she'd changed identities between stops. He was the White Rabbit and she was Alice, a pesky trespasser in his well-ordered universe who might at any moment change size or shape. He didn't stop second-guessing her identity until the church spires of Worms appeared, poking above a sea of squat buildings on a virtually flat landscape. *Worms*, the White Rabbit announced, as the train passed shipyards and warehouses until reaching the center of town.

"You," the conductor addressed Riley in clean, crisp English as the train slowed to a stop. "You get out here." She thanked him with a big smile, to which he only grumbled, "Out! You get out now!" He followed her as she disembarked and then, his job finished, he returned to his well-ordered universe, pocket watch in hand, mouth at the whistle.

CHAPTER 5

HOLY SAND

THE WORMS TRAIN STATION was clean. No graffiti, no trash, no loitering panhandlers begging for money as they did at train stations in the United States. A basic brick and mortar, no frills building, yes. But clean.

Once inside, Riley found a money-exchange office and was attempting to use her German on the clerk to cash a traveler's check when she heard her name. She turned expecting to see her uncle but it was Gil, the driver from the night before. He was taller than she remembered and dressed in grey slacks that fit him well and a crisp periwinkle shirt that complimented his hazel eyes.

"Your uncle's only on his first martini," he explained. "So, he sent me to get you. He's only got an hour for lunch which doesn't leave a lot of time for ..."

"Booze." She said to which he laughed."I'm sorry you had to come get me."

"Well, actually I volunteered."

"Oh."

"How's your first day going so far?" He asked as they walked out to the Volkswagen.

At first she played it cool, answering his questions as succinctly as possible but he was so easy to talk to that soon it all came out: the Putzie and her cleaning fetishes,

the post office which was also the train station and finally, her confusion over the two toilets in her uncle's bathroom. And it came out breathlessly, with no pause or
chance for him to comment. And he just listened as they
drove along until she finally ran out of breath.

"Well, that seals it. You *are* a country bumpkin! The
second toilet is a bidet. It's for washing up that part of
your anatomy *after* you go."

She felt like such an idiot. She'd had three whole
years of German and two of French and not one word in
either class about a bidet, just constant memorization of
stupid scripts, imaginary conversations between you and
your *new* German friend. *Hello, how are you? Let me present
myself. I am Riley. Where is the library, please?*

What a waste.

"I hope you didn't use it for..."

"Oh God, no! I didn't use it at all. I used the bathtub.
Oh golly, not as a toilet! I mean I took a bath. Oh God,
what am I talking about."

"I don't know," he said "But you're charming when
you babble."

Charming when I babble? Then I'm shutting up, she
thought. Charming when I babble — how insulting.

He took the silence following as a chance to play tour
guide.

"Worms is one of the oldest cities in Germany, if not
the oldest, although this fact is disputed by the city Köln,
which also claims the title. See that bridge crossing the
Rhine. That's the Nibelungen Bridge, built originally by
the Romans." He pointed to a bridge not tall nor spec-
tacular but sturdy looking.

"Wow. Really, the Romans? In Reno they tear down old buildings and then they replace them with these god-awful casinos."

"Reno? That's where you're from."

"I'm afraid so."

"Then this must be quite a change for you."

"It's like a different universe."

He laughed. "Ahead of us is Wormser Dom, or Dom Cathedral, where the Edict of Worms was posted. It was the proclamation that—"

"Just because I didn't know what a bidet is, I'm not an idiot. My father's a Lutheran. I just didn't realize Worms was a *place.*"

"Ah. Perhaps you thought the edict had something to do with fishing?"

"Ha, ha. Noooo."

Wormser Dom was constructed of long rectangular blocks that had grown pale peach with age. It lacked the statues of angels and saints and other such finery that the young woman expected from the Catholics, but it was topped by silver-coated turrets that shimmered in the morning sun like a knight's armor. "How do you know so much about Worms? I'd never heard of it before I came here."

"Before I was recruited by Lou Raferman I wanted to teach history, you know, to high school students."

"I can't imagine having a teacher as cute as you. I wouldn't be able to—" Oh God! She thought. How many more stupid things could she possibly say to this man? She changed the subject: "Who's Lou Raferman?"

In profile she could see that the bastard was grinning. "Good question. Oh, on paper he is the chief of operations for the budgeting office, which makes him my boss. And your uncle's. But he's been accused of playing a lot of different roles since the end of the war. He's sort of a chameleon." He rounded a corner. "Soon we'll be passing Heiligen Sand, the oldest Jewish cemetery in Europe. On the right."

There were no polished marble mausoleums, no angel statues, no flowers in the silent untended cemetery they drove past. Many stones had been overturned and lay on their sides in a sea of weeds. Others were slanted sideways or had been chipped. "Why haven't they taken care of this place if it's so famous?" She asked.

"After the war there was no one left to tend the grounds. Any Jew who lived through the Holocaust understandably left soon after."

"But, it was so long ago. Certainly someone has come back."

"It was only twenty-five years ago, and, although that might seem like a long time to you because you're only, what, nineteen?"

"I'm twenty! How old are you? Twenty-five?"

"Twenty-six," he laughed. "Sorry, I didn't mean to insult you. Just wanted to point out that time is relative— you think it's a long time because that's how long you've been around. For countries that have had to rebuild, twenty-five years is just the tip of the iceberg."

Riley seethed inwardly. *Time is relative!* He was talking to her as if she was a stupid child, as if she had no sense of history at all. How smug he was! How sophisticated and cynical! "They could at least try, right?"

He didn't reply as he turned down a freshly asphalted road that led to a compound of modern one-story, red-brick buildings, each with a well marked parking lot to one side and a grass patch in front. "Here we go," he said. "The Officer's Club where you will find your uncle … probably in the bar." He parked the car, handed her the keys and then explained he had to get back to work.

She watched him walk toward another of the many nondescript brick buildings. He's not your type, she told herself and then he turned and winked at her.

You bastard! She mumbled and then she smiled.

CHAPTER 6

THE PROMENADE

THE OFFICERS' CLUB was an oasis of Americana. Just inside the door, a bulletin board announced Luau Night and Indian Chiefs Father/Daughter meetings, along with sign-up sheets for baseball teams. Oh good grief, Riley thought I could be in Topeka, Kansas. You'd think the people stationed here would at least try to assimilate into the German culture!

Beyond the entrance were two rooms: a sunny but almost-empty dining room and a noisy, windowless bar full of smoke where men in uniforms and suits with their shirttails hanging out, bellied up to the bar, chatting with women perched on barstools, their smooth legs crossed as they puffed on ladylike cigarettes and giggled. In the midst of the throng and dressed in a dark suit, stiffly starched white shirt, and dark narrow tie stood her uncle.

"Oh, there's my little niecey now," he said, summoning her over for introductions. His lunch-hour gang consisted of a couple of weary men who, like him, worked for the Army, their much younger wives, a smattering of military types (generals, or colonels or whatever they were) who used Riley's tie-died shirt and thick leather sandals as an excuse to complain about the goddamn hippie peaceniks back in the States. Lastly, and very much out of place, a short, pasty Frenchman whose job description seemed rather vague but who offered Riley the key to his apartment, just in case she needed a place to hang out. He'd heard that all American women were frigid but he kindly gave her the opportunity to prove the rumors false. When she refused the key, he turned his back in a huff.

"Are you hungry?" Uncle Bob finally asked.

"Starving!"

"Okay, then. Let's go to the dining room for some burgers."

Burgers? She thought. I've come all the way to Germany for a burger at an officers' club. Still, she was very hungry.

They'd no sooner sat down when he said:

"Did you see all those young lieutenants at the bar?"

"Yeah."

"Well, I figure that they'd all love to take a pretty American girl out to dinner."

"What?"

"Well, I was thinking, why should I be the one who has to feed you when there are all those young studs who'd gladly—"

"Uncle Bob!"

"You know, you've gotta learn to use what you have while you still have it. Think of it as the law of supply and demand. You've got the supply and they've got the demand," he said, taking a chomp out of a breadstick.

"You want me to lead those guys on so they'll buy me dinner?"

"Yeah, why not? They're lonely. All the German girls are after them, you know, in order to procure an American husband, while you're just over here for a good time.

You don't want a husband, do you?"

"Certainly not! Definitely not someone in the army. Besides, I have a boyfriend!"

"Well, then it's perfect..."

"Uncle Bob! I think you've been with the budget department too long. I'm your niece, and besides, I'm not going to sell myself just for dinner. I didn't come over here to hang out with Americans! I want to meet some real Germans."

"No one said anything about *sex*! I'm sure you know how to get what you want without putting out. All women do."

"Uncle Bob!"

Her burger tasted like it had been frozen for many years, thawed, and then slowly cooked in a dishwasher. There were no frivolous extras such as lettuce, tomato, ketchup, or mustard, but she was hungry and ate, while her uncle ordered yet another Heineken. He was, he explained, on a *special* diet. He would eat very little during the week and then splurge on the weekends. This way he figured he could drink as much as he wanted and not gain weight. Supposedly this diet had worked for him many times in the past. The *drink all you want and eat little during the week and the splurge on the weekend* diet.

"So what are your plans?"

"I just got here. I —"

"No plans." He'd always had plans, he went on to explain. His whole life he'd had plans: to go to college, to get married, to get a job with a guaranteed pension. Boom boom bam. It's what sensible people did.

"I like to take life as it comes. Just go with the flow. See where life leads you. Listen to the universe as it opens doors for you."

"What if no goddamn doors open up?"

The German waitress heard the rising tone of his voice and, thinking he was complaining about her, ran over apologetically with the check. His cheeks turned pink as he mumbled an apology.

When they got back to the bar, the crowd was dispersing, straightening ties, tucking in shirts, and emptying their glasses one last time before they had to go back to the drudgery of work.

Uncle Bob leaned across the bar and summoned the bartender. "Hey, Helmut," he said. "Will you look after my niece for a couple of hours? Riley here doesn't want to hang out with us corrupt Americans. She wants to meet some real Germans."

"Uncle Bob, he has to work!"

"Nah, he's off until 4:30, the start of happy hour! Have her back by then, if you can stand her that long."

Helmut gave Riley the once-over. He had the anguished look of a misunderstood poet, dark hair down to his shoulders, a stubby chin, bags under his eyes. "Naturlich, Herr Neilson," he replied.

"Maybe he has something more important to do, Uncle Bob. I'm not a puppy that needs to be walked!"

"No, no. It will be my pleasure." Helmut insisted.

After her uncle left she said "You really don't have to take me around the city. I'm perfectly capable of exploring the town by myself."

"No. I have promised Herr Neilson and I will do. But I have motorcycle and so we walk or —

"That's great. Back home I have a motorcycle too."

"You have a motorcycle?"

"Yeah, don't girls have motorcycles here in Germany?"

"Of course!" He claimed but she very much doubted him.

"There's not much to do in Worms," He said as she climbed onto the motorcycle behind him and wrapped her arms around his taut midsection."Only a big department store where you can buy things." Americans always want to buy things, he claimed. Things they didn't need. "We will go to the department store," he concluded, "so you could partake in the buying of things you don't need."

"But, I don't have that much money. You know, not all Americans are rich. Besides, I want to do what real Germans would do, not what Americans do. What do Germans do in the afternoon on a day like today?"

He thought a moment. "Real Germans like to walk when the weather is nice. They call it *promenade*."

"Then let's do that. Let's promenade."

For their promenade Helmut chose a popular path than ran along the river. It began just below the old Roman bridge, stretched past barges that had been converted into floating restaurants, and ended in a loop around a modest park. Helmut was quick to point out an apartment complex on the other side of the river where many of the American officers lived because the apartments were equipped with modern appliances and some even had dishwashers. Of course, *real* Germans couldn't afford those places. Real Germans could barely afford a television and had to wait for months just to get a phone line.

But the Americans always demanded and got the best of everything, without even having to wait.

At first Riley concurred with his many anti-American tirades. Yes, Americans were greedy. Yes, Americans were spoiled. Yes, Americans were warmongers. But when he turned every topic into a condemnation of *everything* American, she changed the topic to the odd color of the river. That did the trick. Suddenly the subject became the unclean French, dumping pesticides and industrial waste into the water as it flowed along their shared border. The French had ruined the river. However, he hastened to add, the German government had been able to shame the French into changing their evil ways. Yes, someday there would be fish again and fishing boats and fisherman. But it would take years. Thanks to those unclean French.

"Why don't people smile here?" She asked when he tired of berating the French. She was referring to the wave upon wave of somber pedestrians who responded to her smiles with questioning looks.

"It is not necessary to smile all the time. This is only Americans who do this to show they are good people, and then, such hypocrites, they make the Africans slaves and keep them locked up in the ghettos."

"Well, that's not exactly true. Besides, if you hate Americans, why do you work for them?"

"I am a business student. Someday I will have money and a Lamborghini. I like the Italian cars," Helmut explained. "I only work with Americans to learn better to speak the English. It is very important to speak English well."

"Is it really that bad to work for Americans?".

"No," he replied as they turned stiffly to do another loop on the same path. "Drunken Americans are good tippers."

"Like my uncle?"

"Your uncle only pretends to be drunk. Besides, he works for Lou Raferman."

"Lou Raferman?"

"Yeah, CIA. Spies."

Oh no, she assured him. Her uncle was not a CIA agent but an accountant.

"You are einfältig. What's the English? Clueless." He said and then suggested they round out their afternoon by stopping for coffee near his university. There, he assured the young woman, she would be able to meet other German students.

It was an ambush.

CHAPTER 7

HAPPY HOUR

HAPPY HOUR at the Officer's Club officially began at five o'clock with half price beer on tap and cocktail peanuts set out in bowls, to be kept endlessly full, around the bar. But on Friday, Helmut explained, the regulars always began showing up at least a half hour early demanding service. And they had no restraint. Before the "serious drinking" would even begin, they'd fling their ties and coats unto any nearby table and loosen the collars of their starched white shirts as if they were at home. The young Germans learning to improve their English while tending bar had no choice but to try to keep up with their demands. Friday nights were always the worst.

Having spent the afternoon in a smoky café listening to young Germans tell her just how rotten Americans were, how they kept their former slaves in the ghettos, slaughtered Vietnamese people, and even assassinated their own presidents, Riley was in no mood to join the menagerie at the bar. She hid out in one of the booths the children were relegated to as they stuffed their faces with French fries and pretended to do homework. There she wrote long letters home until her uncle found her.

"What are you thinking?" he whispered. "Look at all the young officers at the bar tonight! Look at all of them!

Certainly one of them live up to your high standards and you can allow him to feed you."

"I'm writing letters home."

"You're such a disappointment to your old unc. At least come up and meet them."

"Okay." She followed him to the bar where Helmut smirked as he filled order after order for the racist war-mongering Americans now getting sloopy drunk and making assholes of themselves. She smiled and made small talk with Sam from Denver and Chris from somewhere in Wisconsin and other young officers whose names she couldn't keep track of. They were light-hearted guys, happy to be stationed in Europe and not in that other place they called "Nam." To her surprise, they were more vehemently opposed to the Vietnam War than the protesters back home. Being stationed in southern Germany was okay; they were close to Paris and the Alps, and—although they didn't use deodorant or shave their armpits—the German girls were awfully friendly. *Wink, wink. If she knew what they meant.*

My poor uncle, she thought. There was no way these guys are going to ask me to dinner and take a chance they might get lucky when there were all those friendly German girls; wink, wink, gorgeous blondes in miniskirts and high-heeled boots, displaying fit thighs and milkmaid breasts, as they tried to decide which young officer would get lucky that evening.

One of them had her eyes on Sam from Denver. My name is Elke, she said. I have an uncle in Chicago. Chicago is wonderful, she said. Was Riley's hometown near

Chicago, she asked.

Not hardly, was the reply.

Then Elke turned to Sam, one hand squeezing his thigh as she asked. "Is Denver near Chicago? Yes, Sam lied, Denver is near Chicago. She'd hooked her dinner date for the night.

CHAPTER 8

THE BIRDCAGE

"SO YOU COULDN'T score a dinner date?" Uncle Bob asked as the officers began departing with their dates. "All those guys and not even a nibble?"

He was sitting next with a woman propped elegantly on the barstool next to him. She had hair the color of copper, short, wavy, and styled to perfection, and a smattering of freckles which swam across her aquiline nose. Her eyes danced when she giggled but otherwise seemed impenetrable.

"Simon, why don't you give my niece some lessons on getting what you want without putting out?"

"*Row-bear!* You are a bad, bad man!" She wore a trim white blouse with a Peter Pan collar, woolen skirt, and a flash of gold at her throat.

"You're French!" Riley said.

She nodded.

The pale man seated on the stool behind her smiled broadly as he reached over to shake Riley's hand. "And I am her husband, Roger Saski, but I'm afraid I am not French!"

41

"And my name is Simone, not *thees* Simon! Your uncle! He insist on calling me 'Simon.'"

"Your old Unc's still got the moves, doesn't he, Niecey? I still know how to woo the ladies."

"Oh yeah, Uncle Bob. You've got the moves." Riley scoffed and then turned to Roger."Where are you from?"

"Detroit, my dear. Detroit."

"Oh, I've been to Detroit!"

At mention of Detroit, Simone bristled."I have *nev-air* been to Detroit. *Raw-jer* will not take me to meet his family."

"Trust me, sweetheart. You don't want to go to Detroit, isn't that right, Riley? The town went for George Wallace in the last election. He's that governor from the South who thinks African Americans shouldn't be allowed in white schools."

"A *tear-eeble* man!"

"Yes, my dear, terrible. And that is why we do not return. Oh, look. There's Annie."

A tall blonde had spotted them from across the room. She smiled, waved and then joined them. After a bit of nervous small talk she said: "Bob, I need to talk you about something."

"Of course." He followed her to a shadowy corner of the room where they stood talking.

Simone and her husband exchanged worried glances as if they knew what was going on. And then they turned to Riley all smiles.

"There are other places in the United States that aren't so — "

"It wasn't a matter of not wanting to return to the States. Simone's family is here and I knew she wouldn't be happy living any other place," he sighed, glancing at his watch. "Speaking of which, Maman has undoubtedly finished her cassoulet and is wondering where we are."

"Ah, yes. Maman. I'm sorry we must leave you. My mother she is visiting. But we will see you again." She climbed down from her perch and gave Riley a perfumed kiss on both cheeks. "This is how we say hello and good-bye in France."

They motioned their departure to the few remaining Friday night celebrants and then exited the officers' club. They were soon followed by others until the bar was almost empty, but still her uncle and Annie remained deep in conversation. Riley, who was so exhausted she didn't care if dinner was the remainder of the peanut butter sandwich she'd made that morning, considered interrupting them. *Please I'm so tired. Have some pity on me.* But before she could, a gruff-looking man grabbed Annie's arm, said something to her and then escorted her out the door.

Her uncle stood in the corner for a few moments with his head down before returning to the bar. "You got rid of the Saskis pretty quick. What did you say?"

"Her mother was making them dinner."

"Ah yes, I forgot she was visiting. Helmut, another Heineken, por favor."

Helmut picked up the peanut bowl and hid it beneath the counter. "Ist seven o'clock. Happy hour is ended."

"Seven o'clock? Crap! I was supposed to be at Lou's a half hour ago. Niecey, where's the car?"

"In the parking lot."

"I sure hope you don't drive like your mother."

"We're not going home? I'm so tired."

"It'll be a quick stop. You can wait in the car."

* * *

Lou Raferman lived on the top floor of a V-shaped build-ing near the cathedral she and Gil had passed earlier in the day. It had been constructed of the same heavy gran-ite blocks, probably during the same era, but had no windows or welcoming bric-brac of any sort.

"People actually live here? It looks like a jail." Riley asked as they crossed the poorly lit and unfurnished lob-by to something resembling a human sized bird cage.

"Lou does. I'm not sure about anybody else. I don't ask. Climb in."

"You've got to be kidding."

"It's a perfectly safe lift, as they call them...if you hold your breath. You can hold your breath for a few minutes, can't you?"

"Very funny," Riley said stepping into the cage.

"Hold your breath now!" He said flipping the switch

As the cable pulled them tenuously upward, Riley's mind flashed to the scene in the movie *Charade* where Audrey Hepburn was trapped in such a lift and threat-ened by Lee Marvin. Or was it George Kennedy? She couldn't remember.

"Wouldn't the stairs be safer?"

"I don't think so. They're very old and not well main-tained."

"On purpose?"

"Probably."

She began to think that Helmut was right. There had to be something sinister about this Lou Raferman. Who else would live in a fortress like building by himself with unsafe stairs and an ancient elevator? But the man who greeted them once they got to the third floor looked more like Truman Capote than Sean Connery. This is the man everyone's so afraid of, she thought as he shook her hand. "Ah, Riley Anne. Aren't you lovely? Of course you must call me Uncle Lou. Come into my parlor," he said, leading then into a room whose waist-to-ceiling plate glass windows framed the lights of the city.

"I couldn't get rid of her for the night. No buyers." Her uncle said. "I tried. I said, 'Niecey, just be nice to one of those nice young officers. You don't gotta give out the goods,' but no. She doesn't take after her mother, that's for sure. My sis always knew how to…"

"That's not a problem, Robert. Gilbert, you don't mind showing our guest around while I deal with her uncle, do you?

Gil rose from a high-back chair facing the windows. In the softly lit room, he seemed less boy-next-door and more film noir detective. He even had a five o'clock shadow.

Riley felt light-headed. "That's alright, Mr. Raferman. I can just wait here. He doesn't have to…he's already —"

"It's not a problem." Gil said.

"But…"

"For heaven's sakes. You don't have to sleep with the

man. He's just gonna show you around."

"Uncle Bob!"

"Then that's settled," Lou said. "End of discussion. Would you like something to eat, my dear? I can have my maid make you something."

"No thanks. I've eaten far too many French fries and peanuts at the officers' club."

Lou patted his stomach, "You must watch those *Pommes frites*, my dear. They'll sneak up on you." Then he ushered Uncle Bob into the brightly lit kitchen and closed the door tight.

"Come here and look at the view," Gil said. "I don't bite."

"I'm sorry you've gotten stuck with me again. I just couldn't wait in the car in some dark alley the way my uncle expected me to."

"What makes you think I mind? You sure are a funny one."

The room Lou referred to as his parlor sat at the tip of the V. To the right lay the sleeping center of town. To the left, the river, where restaurant barges twinkled as they bobbed under the ghostly bridge. There was no Army issue furniture in Lou Raferman's apartment but instead, Oriental rugs, antique hutches, overstuffed leather couches and curios filled with ivory carvings. On the walls were paintings of beautiful young men gazing soulfully into each other's eyes and English hunting scenes. Riley asked if the boys in the paintings were Lou's sons and Gil laughed. Lou Raferman had never been married and never would be, at least in the twentieth century. He preferred the company of men, young men.

"Helmut the bartender thinks that Lou Raferman is

the head of the CIA!"

"The Germans think that all the DACs work for the CIA, pretty much in the way that Americans believe that all Germans were Nazis," he explained as they walked out to the balcony. "And, to be honest, Lou does nothing to discredit that myth. I think he likes being thought of as dangerous."

From Lou's balcony the riverboat scene below looked so inviting, people enjoying a calm night, drinking, eating and laughing as classical music played. They quietly enjoyed the scene for a few minutes and then Gil began:"I bet you're exhausted. Jet lag takes a few days to recover from."

"It's just that nothing is —"

"Like you expected, right?"

"That's for sure."

"You should extend your stay in Europe—take a year or so off from college. You'd learn so much more—"

He spotted something behind her.

Lou Raferman stood watching them, a long ribbon of smoke circling like a question mark above his head. "A romantic sight, the river boats. You'll have to come again. But it's late and your uncle's ready to be transported home."

"Thanks, Mr. Raferman."

"Of course, you'll have to extract him from a very unnecessary nightcap."

She found her uncle sitting at a small table in a kitchen so white and bright that it hurt her eyes. Across the table from him sat a gloomy man who hadn't even looked up when she'd entered. "Uncle Bob,"she said, as her uncle threw back his head and inhaled the drink he'd been holding. "How am I going to find my way home if you pass out?"

"I can take you both home." Gil offered.

"Don't you have to catch a train to Rotterdam tonight?"

"It's not until midnight, Lou."

"You're going to Holland?"

"My home base is here but I travel a lot. Maybe sometime you can—"

"Miss O'Tannen will be just fine. Take the road in front of this building toward the river. Until you get to B47. Then turn right. Just make sure that you head north on B47, toward Mainz, and not south. After about 20 minutes (depending on how fast you drive) you'll see the sign for Gunthersblum. If you get lost, pull over and ask for help from one of the numerous *polizei* who will be trailing you. They know the route."

"You're kidding?"

"I'm afraid not. They'd love nothing better than to catch your uncle driving with a suspended license so they can throw him in the brig. That's why you're here, my dear. To make sure that doesn't happen."

"You haven't seen the way she drives! I'd be safer in the brig. Far safer! Isn't that right, Niecey?"

"I usually don't have to find my way around a strange town being guided by a drunk —"

"What a way to speak to your uncle. See what I have to put up with, Lou?"

"I see what *she* has to put up with, Robert."

Shortly after finding the road heading north to Mainz, Uncle Bob passed out. His head slipped against the side window and moments later he was snoring. Riley followed B47 out of Worms, past dark fields and factories, through silent villages. She didn't see any other cars. No one followed her. She was sobbing when she finally reached the turnoff for Gunthersblum. The day had been far too long. Far too full of new faces and perspectives. Far too much. The next day being Saturday she hoped to sleep and sleep and sleep. But that was not to be.

CHAPTER 9

POFFY DOFFY

SLOOP, SLOOP, SLOOP...CLUNK, CLUNK.Sloop, sloop, sloop...clunk, clunk.

The sound woke her from restless dreams.

Sloop, sloop, sloop...clunk, clunk.

The sky was still dark and the village, still.

Sloop, sloop, sloop...clunk, clunk.

Perhaps it's bad plumbing, Riley thought, or the old refrigerator in the kitchen.

Sloop, sloop, sloop...clunk, clunk.

It was no use. She couldn't get back to sleep, even with a pillow over her head and the door shut. The noise was right beneath her, taunting her. And so she slipped a blanket over her shoulders and followed the sound downstairs to the living room. There, stretched to full length on the La-Z-Boy lay her uncle sound asleep. Only he was not alone. A fat yellow cat had taken up residence on his lap and from the look on its face, the young woman was not welcome.

Sloop, sloop, sloop.

The culprit was a record spinning on the turntable next to her uncle, its needle stuck in the groove of an oft-played tune. She moved the needle. The song continued.

Looking back,
Perhaps she's been,
The only human thing

That ever gave back love to me.

The record ended, the needle lifted, the turntable stopped spinning, and it was quiet. For a second.

"Oh, Sloopy. That damn cat," her uncle mumbled, one hand resting in the fur of the cat, the other still wrapped around an almost empty glass.

What is this sentimental sloop? Riley thought, picking up the record jacket from the floor. *Stanyan Street and Other Sorrows.* Poetry? Uncle Bob?

"That damn cat," he mumbled again. She carefully removed the glasses from the end of his nose and put them on top of a half-done puzzle page. Then she turned off the light and stumbled back upstairs in the dark. But she couldn't stop thinking about the events of the day, about how nothing had turned out as she expected. Her uncle didn't even seem to want her around, except to appease his boss and keep him out of a German jail. What a mistake it had been to come over to Europe with no plans, only some romantic illusions about how every-thing would turn out. Uncle Bob was right; she was an idiot. In the morning she would make plans to return home.

But the next morning she found her uncle freshly showered and shaved as he read the *Stars and Stripes* and drank his coffee.

"Uncle Bob, you look so nice!"

"Is that right? Didn't your mother ever tell you it is a sin to lie?"

"I'm not lying. You look a whole lot nicer than you did a little while ago. You even smell nice."

"Well, I won't argue with you there. Hey, did you steal

my puzzles?"

"Yup and I solved the cipher that you got stuck on. It was something silly, like *Since the masseur was not making enough money he kneaded some new clients.* The trick word was 'kneaded.'"

"Kneaded? I probably would have gotten that eventually, if I wasn't living with a puzzle thief!"

"Sorry. I needed something to help me get back to sleep. Last night was so —"

"What do you say, since it's Saturday, we take a drive over to France for lunch?"

Riley's resolve to return home immediately evaporated. "France? Are you kidding? Of course." She was ready to go and in the car in less than five minutes.

He laughed when he saw her behind the wheel, anxious and as giddy as a child going to Disneyland. *Yippee, France, yippee.*

* * *

They took the backroads to France, passing through villages unaffected by the war while others had been partially if not totally rebuilt. "What a shame that they're not rebuilding these villages to look like they did before the war. The new buildings look so blah and uninteresting next to the old ones."

"Wars have a funny way of bankrupting countries, Riley. The survivors needed places to live and work and they needed them sooner, rather than later, which didn't leave a lot time for...aesthetics. Besides, the thatched cottages you see in the movies weren't that charming to the people who actually had to live in them."

She was quiet after that. Of course, he was right. They were passing through an area which had been bombed; where people had fought and died and those who'd survived had to go on. She remembered what Helmut had said about the apartments built for American officers which had all the modern amenities an ordinary German could only dream about. It didn't seem fair and yet most of the officers she'd talked to would much rather be home than have all those perks. It didn't seem fair on either side.

* * *

At Saarbrucken they crossed over into France, stiffly questioned by German guards who clicked their knee-high boots and demanded to see their passports, her international drivers' license, and even the car's insurance papers. While at the French border, the shorter, livelier guards merely waved them through.

To Riley, crossing the border between the two countries was like watching a black and white movie suddenly burst into color. More people seemed to be out on the streets, chatting, riding bikes, laughing. The flowers seemed to bloom more profusely and in a more dazzling array of colors. The sky even seemed to have lightened to a brighter shade of blue.

She shared this observation with her uncle.

"Is that a fact?"

"Don't you think it's strange that the people in two

countries can live side by side and be so different?"

"The United States is not at all like Mexico. And we live side by side."

"Ah, but that's different. How can countries living side by side for *centuries* be so different?"

Her uncle's mind was elsewhere. "You don't say," he said to close a discussion he obviously felt wasn't worth pursuing.

"Where are we going?"

"Poffy Doffy."

"Poffy Doffy? What's that?"

"You'll see," he said before slipping back within himself.

On the outskirts of Sarreguemines, he ordered her to slow down and then stop by the side of the road. "The turn off is somewhere along here," he said as he climbed out of the car and began looking for some sign amidst the trees that crowded toward them like curious undertakers.

"Here? Are you sure? I don't see anything."

"That's by design. Here it is." He pointed to a one lane road leading into the dark woods. It was guarded by a simple wooden gate which now lay open.

"Okay" she said as he climbed back into the car. "but it's such a narrow road."

"You won't be running into any cars driving in the opposite direction. At least, not for a couple of hours."

"I certainly hope not."

Soon they were in the midst of a forest so thick that little light managed to twinkle through the canopy and she was forced to turn on the headlights. "Are you sure?" She asked again as the road beneath them turned to gravel.

"Keep going." Deeper and deeper into this forest they crept until they reached the end of the road. There, fashionably dressed people, many wearing wide-brimmed sun hats or jaunty fedoras, had abandoned their vehicles and were following a foot path leading further into the woods.

We can't be going to the same place as those people, the Riley thought, as they parked the car and followed along. She wore a peasant skirt and blouse and her uncle, a Polo shirt and shorts and neither wore a hat. But he didn't seem at all self-conscious.

Before long they emerged from the dark and silent woods into a park-like clearing filled with sunlight and the sound of violins. There, across a sea of grass, well manicured and dewy in the midday sun, stood an alabaster chateau and, beside the chateau, a pond large enough to host a flotilla of white swans.

"This is like a secret castle in a fairy tale," Riley whispered, "What's the history of this place?"

"You have to try the escargot,"

"What?"

"The snails."

Adjacent to the water dozens of waiters were busy setting up white-clothed tables and chairs as if for an impromptu luncheon.

"They're not so bad. They taste a bit like buggers, nice and salty."

"Oh gross!"

A maître d' in a formal tux greeted them as they neared the tables. "Nielson. *Un* table pour three people, pour *favora.*" Uncle Bob said.

The man winced but, after checking his list of antici-pated attendees, led them toward a table on the lake's edge.

"Mon amori et arrivez, toutie sweet."

"*Très bonn*, monsieur."

"Uncle Bob, what language are you speaking, because I had a year of French in junior high and—"

"Niecey dear, they understand me and you know why? I speak the universal language: money."

"I don't think that kind of attitude—" The lecture she an-ticipated giving her uncle on proper behavior in a foreign country would have to wait. His broad Swedish face be-gan to glow like the early morning sun. "Uncle Bob?"

Simone, the French wife of his co-worker, had emerged from the dark woods, smiling as the maître d' rushed to greet her. Unable or unwilling to wait, Uncle Bob leapt from his seat with a gasp as though temporarily frozen by the sight of her. This sudden motion in such a sublime setting roused the interest of the other diners and the waiters. They all turned to witness Riley's uncle sprinting across the grass toward Simone.

She greeted him with cheek kisses and then giggled like a school girl with a crush as he grasped her arm and gal-lantly led her back to the table. The crowd broke into ap-plause. *Ooh la la, amour.* He gave a little bow and then they sat down.

"You remember Simon from the officers' club."

"Simone!" She kissed Riley on both cheeks, and sat down. "How do you like Le Petit Dauphin?"

"Oh, it's beautiful. Really beautiful."

"Your uncle call *zeez* place 'Poffy Doffys."

"Yes, he likes to make up his own words!"

"Can you tour the chateau?"

She shook her head. "Oh no. C'est impossible."

"Really?"

"Oui. It is ... private, you see."

Riley had even more questions but Simone changed the subject. "Are you prepare for the fests?"

"The fests?"

"Certainement your uncle take you to fest. The fest-hopping, it is a passion?"

"Tomorrow she'll be driving Charlie and me."

"Oh, mon dieu, not Charlie Newsome!"

"Who's Charlie Newsome?"

"You met him last night at Lou's. Unfortunately, Old Charlie's also had some run-ins with the *polizei*. Suspended driver's license."

The only thing Riley remembered from the night before was the long-faced man puffing on a cigarette at Lou's kitchen table.

"What's wrong with Charlie Newsome?"

"He has much sadness.Do not let him drink too much around these Germans."

"That's the purpose of the fests. To drink the local wine and beer. To eat bratwurst smothered in onions, dance the polka with the *frauleins*. Simon here doesn't like the nasty old fests, but you'll have fun. You'll get to meet lots of *real* Germans."

Sure, Riley thought. What twenty-year-old girl wouldn't want to drive a couple of middle-aged men from village to village while they drank beer and made fools of themselves? Still, she would get to see the countryside and the local villages.

"This is not a good idea. You cannot trust *thees* man around the Germans."

"It'll be fine. My niece can handle it."

"I can?"

As each course came and went, the lovers giggled …. about the perfect weather … about his mangling of languages … about her freckles … anything and everything. They barely touched their food which Riley found unfathomable. How was it possible to be so in love that you couldn't take the time to enjoy your chocolate mousse? Finally only coffee remained and she did not drink coffee so she took one of the many not so subtle hints that her uncle had been dropping and announced she was taking a walk. And, she got the response she expected: *good, good and take your time. Take at least an hour!*

She meandered along a lakeside path that eventually led to the far side of the lake. She could no longer hear the violins or the chatter of the diners. Just the honking of the swans as they squabbled. There she found a trail into the woods that looked inviting. As she passed the ferns and vine-covered logs, the white lilies gossiping in the shadows, the benches set aside for lovers, she imagined knights in shining silver armor riding through those same magical woods. Maybe even Joan of Arc with her armies.

The man walking in front of her had the same frame as Gil, broad-shoulders, narrow hips and long legs making her feel even more alone. She wondered if she'd ever see Gil again or if he'd only been so kind and gentle because he felt protective. He probably had a dozen girlfriends; one in every port as they say. Each one infinitely better dressed and more sophisticated than Riley O'Tannen, the dewey-eyed idiot from the hick town of Reno Nevada.

The man stopped. She did too. He drew a cigarette and lit it in silhouette. He had a Roman nose and a low hairline, his lips were thick and pouty. He turned and pondered Riley with a leer. Suddenly the forest lost its magic.

When she returned to the table by the lake, her uncle was sitting by himself. A bell rang and the guests rose from their seats almost in unison and, after collecting their things, began heading back to their cars. It was as if they were actors in a play who'd just been given the direction to exit Stage Right. As each group departed, the staff cleared their table and then folded it for storage. It was only four in the afternoon but already long shadows fell across the clearing from the thick, strange woods to the west.

As they walked back toward their car, Riley turned to view Poffy Doffy one last time. All of the tables were gone, presumably loaded into the small van now making its way back towards the darkening chateau. The swans huddled at the end of the lake as though also preparing to be stored in a prop room.

They drove home as though returning from a funeral.

Riley didn't ask her uncle why he was seeing a married French lady, knowing that if she had, he certainly would have told her that it was none of her business. She wondered if she would ever see Le Petit Dauphin again or if, like Brigadoon, it only appeared every thirty years for one afternoon in early September.

That evening she sat in one of the Army-issue green foam chairs, studying maps of the area, as her uncle drank scotch, did crossword puzzles, and then fell asleep in the recliner with the big yellow cat on his lap.

In the wee hours of the morning, she again heard Rod McKuen calling for his missing cat, "sloop, sloop, sloop..." and went down to move the needle to another groove.

CHAPTER 10

FEST HOPPING

THE NEXT MORNING Riley awoke to the rat-a-tat of voices coming from downstairs. What on earth's going on, she thought as she dressed and ran down to investigate.

The kitchen was full of villagers, all clamoring around her uncle. Some of them she recognized—Heinrich from the train station/post office and the elderly couple who lived across the street. But most of them she had never seen before. After exchanging happy banter with her uncle and slapping him on the back, they each grabbed either a carton of cigarettes, a tin of coffee, a jar of peanut butter or some other American delicacy before leaving.

"How did you get all this stuff?" She asked, after making her way over to him.

"I saved up unused ration cards from people who've been transferred stateside. This stuff is too expensive for my buddies here," he said, turning to the older woman who lived across the street. "Omie, here, just loves Rocky Road ice cream. Don't you, Omie."

Omie grabbed the container he'd pulled from the freezer. "Danke, Oncle Boob!" She smiled and then quickly made her way out the front door as if someone else might be interested in the coveted prize.

"Thanks to you I seem to have a new moniker: Oncle

Boob! Makes me sound a bit like the village idiot, doesn't it?"

She mumbled an apology but couldn't help but giggle herself. Oncle Boob! It was just too appropriate!

* * *

The giveaway lasted about an hour with everyone getting something and everyone leaving happy. Riley thought it was an auspicious start to the day but her uncle did not share her optimism: "Newsome's going to ruin everything! He was supposed to be here an hour ago."

Her uncle had meticulously drawn out their route on a map of all the local fests that he'd gone to *great* pains to acquire. Then he'd rated each and every one in case they weren't able to attain his ultimate goal which was: visiting them all. The prize being — bragging rights at the officers club. A great honor indeed and one which had been his, on many occasions. On his map, the *Must Visit* fests were circled in red while the *Nice to Visits* were circled in blue. Each fest was also given a priority level of one through five.

"I'd better reassess my plans," he complained after another half hour passed. He pulled out the map and began studying his fest-hopping strategy with all the seriousness of a four star general planning a sneak attack against a much better equipped enemy. "The Leusdorf fest will have to be downgraded to a four. It's too far east. We couldn't possibly swing back to Klingerbrick and still make Rheinfell. Goddamnit Newsome! It's almost eleven!"

Just when it looked like her uncle's assault on Rheinfell was in jeopardy, Charlie Newsome appeared, perched precariously on an antique motor scooter that he could barely handle. "Look what I'm reduced to, Bob. A goddamned motor scooter. I can't even remember which of the exes left this pile of *merde* behind on her way out."

But Uncle Bob wasn't in the mood for idle chitchat. The campaign was already an hour behind schedule. "Put that ugly thing around back and get in the damn car," he said, pulling the front seat of the VW forward.

"In the back? It's smaller than a shoe box."

"That's right but Niecey here has to drive. God help us. She can barely keep the car on the road but, Lou will shoot us both if we get caught driving again."

"I think he'd consider a firing squad too light a punishment."

Charlie scrunched in behind Riley, his knees folded up to his chin as he sat sideways on the hard seat. He was a tall and lanky man with straight black hair, made shiny by goo that no longer properly did its job.

They stopped at each of the fests only long enough to be friendly and to sample a few wines and beers. Then it was back into the car to crisscross paths with gangs of fest-hopping college kids and American soldiers. Uncle Bob joined in with the crowds, laughing and joking, while Charlie drank solemnly off to the side. He smirked at the white bratwurst, smothered in sauerkraut and pungent onion rings, which were a staple at each fest. "They look like giant penises" he said. He complained about the beer, the wine, the cheap and shoddy goods sold by elderly women. Everything about fests seemed to put him in an uglier and uglier mood.

* * *

By the end of the afternoon they still had several villages remaining on their list, including one "Must." But the sun was now a memory and the autumn air was nippy, especially for Uncle Bob who was dressed in shorts and sandals. Sadly, he folded his map, but the day was not over. The most important fest, the big one, awaited. The Worms fest where there would be a large circus tent, bands, singing, dancing, and plenty of beer.

"I'm not the man I once was, Niecey," He complained as they drove into Worms. "When I was younger, I could have done them all, all the villages and the big one in Worms too. But I'm an old man now—almost thirty-six!"

Charlie groaned from his scrunched-up position in the back. "Try being almost sixty."

CHAPTER 11

LUSTIG IST DAS ZIGEUNERLEBEN

Lustig ist das Zigeunerleben, faria, faria, ho.
Brauch'n dem Kaiser kein Zins zu geben, faria, faria,ho.
Lustig ist es im grünen Wald
wo des Zigeuners Aufenthalt. Faria, faria, faria, faria, faria,
faria, ho!

SIMONE HAD NOT overstated the danger of exposing Charlie Newsome to crowds of happy Germans. Once inside the massive tent where the main festival was being held, Charlie had quickly sickened at the sight of so many happy Germans waving their beer steins as they swayed to the polka music. He spotted members of the French garrison huddled scornfully in a corner of the tent and insisted upon joining them.

After a few minutes of enduring their dark mood and red wine, Uncle Bob went in search of a "beer wench" from whom to buy a couple of pitchers of beer. Riley watched her uncle schmooze his way through the crowds and knew he probably wouldn't return voluntarily.

The Frenchmen, like Charlie, were disgusted by everything. The wine was disgusting! The beer was disgusting! The food was beyond disgusting! They hunched together, smoking and smoking and smoking as they growled.

Without warning the music stopped. The crowd

hummed in anticipation as all eyes focused on the band platform. What was going on? Who'd dared to interrupt the fest merriment? Whispers and mumbles soon filled the tent as the lead singer, a bearded man looking rather silly in lederhosen and a Pinocchio hat, stepped to the microphone to plead for silence. Then he began speaking solemnly.

"What's he saying?" Riley asked.

"He's introducing the burgermeister," Charlie said slamming his stein down on the wood-plank table. "It's Kert Dradon! We should have hung that damned Nazi when we had the chance. If I'd only known … if I'd only known! But I was a young fool in love, just trying to make sense of things that made no sense. It all happened too fast, goddamn it. We should have killed him when we had the chance."

A man at the next table turned toward Charlie: *Shhh!* he warned As soon as his back was turned, Charlie stuck out his tongue. The spotlight shone on the burgermeister, dressed in the traditional Nieblingen outfit, complete with Viking horns. He lifted his stein to the audience and began pompously addressing the crowd. There was groaning, considerable shushing, and finally, applause when he sat down in his throne-like chair. The music began again, as did the merriment.

"*Quelle* idiot!" One of the French soldiers snorted in disgust.

Charlie reached behind Riley and roughly nudged the man who'd shushed him, causing the man to drop his beer onto the sawdust floor. The man glanced around puzzled, and then, assuming it was an accident, picked up his stein from the floor, refilled it from the pitcher on the table, and continued singing and swaying as though nothing was amiss.

Lustig ist es im grunen Wald

"Bloody murderers! Bloody, goddamn Nazi butcherers."

Wo des Zigeuners Aufenthalt

The French soldiers exchanged glances. One of them reached out to Charlie who jerked away from him and climbed onto the table. "Goddamn Nazi bastards. I've seen what you did! I was there!"

Faria, faria, ho! Ho, ho, ho.

"Sit down Charlie," Riley pleaded as the French soldiers debated whether or not to flee out the back. But Charlie ignored them all. He grabbed the Frenchmen's pitcher of beer and threw it at the next table, barely missing one of the women and splattering them all with beer.

"Goddamn Nazi bastards! I saw what you did!" He cried, tears running down his gaunt cheeks.

The polka band stopped. Men from the surrounding tables slowly stood and started towards Charlie. The French soldiers also rose. One of them pointed a finger at his temple. "*Verruckte,*" he said pointing at Charlie. Crazy.

Charlie slumped from the table and into the arms of two of the Frenchmen. The others quickly flagged a beer wench and promised to buy pitchers of beer for the people at the table Charlie'd attacked. "We're leaving," they promised. That seemed to satisfy the mob, at least momentarily.

"Damnit Newsome," Uncle Bob scowled when he finally arrived on the scene, "I'd just found myself a date for the night. Why did you have to go and start World War III? See that *fraulein* with the huge juggers? She was putty in my hands, putty in your old unc's hands, Niecey."

"I've seen what these people are capable of. I was one of the first to see! God help me. Piles of bodies. Those poor souls still alive, looking more corpse-like than the dead. God help me, I can't get the picture out of my head. And it was him, Bob. It was him!" Charlie sobbed, as they pulled him out of the tent.

The streets were now foggy and dark, the walk back to the car, long and cold. *Lustig ist das Zeigeunerleben* echoed against the walls of the medieval town.

"Did you see those juggers? I coulda been nuzzling those beauts by now, grasping that fanny and listening to my little piggy snort with delight. But you had to go and have some damn existential moment, Newsome!"

Poor Charlie seemed torn between apologizing and breaking into fresh sobs. He lagged behind them, head down.

"Yes sir, I could've had some night!"

"Uncle Bob, you're so gross."

"No, he's right—" Charlie began.

"The war was over at least twenty-five years ago," Riley.said. "We're friends with Germany now."

"You'll learn one day that twenty years is nothing," Charlie sobbed, his eyes dark saucers in the lamplight.

CHAPTER 12

SECRETS FROM THE CELLAR

THE ONLY THING super about the Super Mart in Gunthersblum was the man who simultaneously loaded the outdoor vegetable and fruit cart and manned the antique cash register inside.

Riley had awoken the morning after the fests with a splitting headache. The polka music ringing in her ears, the smoky tent, and the memory of Charlie Newsome sobbing as they drove him home—all had kept her tossing restlessly for most of the night.

By the time she got downstairs, her uncle had already left for work. She searched the kitchen. She searched the bathroom. She even searched the liquor cabinet but she couldn't find any sort of painkiller. She had no choice but to walk downtown to the only store in town and pray they had something to help her..

"Bitte. Wo ist die aspirin?" She asked, once she was able to get the clerk's attention.

Aspirin? Was ist?

She pointed to her head and groaned.

"Kopfschmerzen!" He led her to the Apotheke section and then left her to attend to another customer.

Some help she thought as she picked through the bottles of pills trying to read the labels. It was hopeless. They were all in German, only German. If she bought the wrong thing, she could kill herself. Another complaint to add to her list for Herr Assmus. Why hadn't he taught them how to buy aspirin at a drug store? It was certainly more important than learning, well, for one thing, how to find the frigging library! She wondered what he would say. He was such a peculiar man, more spider than human, prickly, nervous and prone to sneezing attacks. The incarnation of Ichabod Crane! But someone had to speak up, lest one of his students pooped in the bidet or took the wrong drug and died.

She was so busy mentally lecturing Herr Assmus that she didn't realize she was being watched.

"Pardon. You are American?"

She turned to the couple standing stoically behind her.

"We are brother and sister," the young German woman said. "My brother cannot speak English like me."

He, the brother, nodded with a shy grin. They didn't look like siblings; she had thick curly hair the color of tree bark and sturdy farm legs while he was tall and gangly.

"Where in States you come from?" she asked.

"Reno, Nevada."

"Nevada?"

"It's near California. You know—it's where they film *Bonanza*. Virginia City, Lake Tahoe, Little Joe?" Riley had seen reruns of Bonanza on German TV so she was fairly confident they'd recognize the name.

"*Bonanza*?" The brother asked. "Little Joe? Hoss?

"Yup. Virginia City is close to where I live."

"It is dangerous, right? The savage Indians?"

"Not any more. The Indians in Nevada were never that savage. It was the white man..." Riley realized that she'd lost them both and so went on to other topics less socio-political.

Not only did they help her buy the right pain killer but they tagged along with her the rest of the day. He was on leave from the army, and she had the week off from her job at a department store in the nearby city of Mainz. It didn't take long before she realized that, unlike Helmut's comrades who'd dwelt endlessly on American atrocities, they had no desire to debate the great moral dilemmas of their time. In fact, they had no aspirations other than to live in Gunthersblum for the rest of their lives and in their parent's house as there was zero prospect of own-ing their own. They were so different from the kids she'd grown up with. Hopeful for so little; just a life at least as comfortable as their parents. No lofty ideals or ambi-tions, no political opinions (all politics and politicians were the same and corrupt), no expectations of cars, tele-visions, extravagant vacations—just a simple life. It de-pressed Riley to see people her age without the hunger to change the world or to rise up the ladder to what those in America defined as success; more money, more power; greater knowledge than our parents. But, on the other hand, they seemed happy, content, and secure, on a path that wouldn't lead to an uncomfortable place. If she dared tell her parents: "I just want to live with you the rest of my life, work in the local store, maybe travel a bit," they'd blow a gasket.

That night Riley proudly told her uncle she'd made a couple of new friends and he didn't have to worry about entertaining her (not that he ever did). She thought he'd at least pretend to be impressed but he just looked at her and said, "Cripes, what do you have in common with those two? Nothing."

"Well, for one thing, I'll have someone to go out with at night. You don't have to worry about always being stuck with me."

"Yes, but why not one of the teachers at the American school? They're young …"

"They're not Germans."

"Suit yourself then."

Her new friends soon introduced her to the nightlife in Mainz, a city about the same size as Worms but with a hipper, more modern vibe, where young people from the nearby villages and towns danced until sweaty under disco balls. The smoke and body odor inside those clubs was so dense she could hardly breathe, the noise level so deafening that her ears rang the next day, but she had fun. By the end of that week she'd gotten so chummy with the brother and sister that they insisted she come to their house for lunch. She was delighted.

"Isn't that wonderful?" She told her uncle. "They like me!"

"It's not a good idea to become chummy with the villagers."

"Well, you're friendly with them."

"I don't go to their houses for lunch."

"Why not?"

"Just remember that I warned you."

She couldn't imagine what her uncle had against the villagers. Just because they weren't as well educated or worldly as his friends didn't mean that they wouldn't make good friends. And so she ignored him and on the day of the lunch, flowers in hand, she cheerfully showed up at the home of the brother and sister.

They lived not far from her uncle in a half-timber in the older section of town. It looked charming and quaint on the outside, but inside, the ceilings were low and the windows too small to let in much light. The parents greeted her awkwardly. Neither spoke English. Both had thick hands roughened by years of hard work and smiled very little. For lunch they served a potato stew with a wide swath of fat floating on top, followed by crunchy sugar cake and honey-sweetened black tea. As they ate, the father asked Riley questions in German, translated to English by the sister. Where did she come from in America? How long was she staying? Etc cetera. The mother said nothing as did the brother. Finally the father asked a question that his daughter did not want to translate.

"Nein, Papa."

"What is it? I'll answer any questions."

"No. He wants to show you a thing."

Now she was really curious. "No, it's okay. Really." She imagined he was a whittler, like so many of the villagers, and that he carved awkward figurines the brother and sister found embarrassing. "Really, he can show me anything."

The sister exchanged a few words with her brother. He said, "Warum nichts?" *Why not.*

73

"Yeah, ist gut," Riley said directly to the father. He smiled, displaying cracked and yellowed teeth, and then left the room as the mother began clearing the table with the help of her children. Riley was not permitted to help and ordered to stay seated.

After a short time, the father returned, carefully setting an intricately carved mahogany box down on the table. First, he unlocked the sacred box and removed a roll of black velvet, which he spread carefully over the table, straightening the edges so that it would lay flat. After satisfied the velvet was flat enough to showcase his pride and joy, he pulled forth several brass pins with the emblem of an eagle, wings spread, and carrying in its talons a silver swastika. But that was not all! Oh no, he also had a collection of iron crosses with tiny swastikas in the middle. Ribbons and medals, the sister translated, for valor and loyalty. Once finished he pulled his shoulders back and looked as though he was about to shout "Heil Hitler!"

Riley opened her mouth and from her frozen brain sprang forth the phrase that she'd been mentally rehearsing: "Sehr schön."

The sister looked stunned as did the brother.

"Sehr schön," the father repeated. "Yeah!" Then he went on in German, which the sister translated: "What a shame that, because of a ban on hoarding Nazi memorabilia, I must hide these things in the cellar."

What a shame, she agreed.

* * *

On the drive home from happy hour that night Uncle Bob chuckled at her story. What did she expect? Under Hitler, times were good for many Germans. All they had to do was pretend that the camps didn't exist.

"It's been so many years. They've got to know by now what really happened."

"They're just townsfolk. Besides they don't cover the Holocaust in German schoolbooks. They don't want to traumatize the younger generation."

"That's terrible!"

"That's just the way it is. Anyway, I have a surprise that might cheer you up."

"Oh yeah?"

"You're going to Italy."

"What? Italy? Really?"

"Yup, you're going to take old Charlie down to pick up his car."

Her happy bubble burst. "You're kidding. That guy's crazy. He almost got us killed!"

"He's harmless. He only goes bananas in crowds of singing Germans. Besides, don't you think you've gotten enough cultural stimulation from the Gunthersblumians? Don't you want to see Switzerland and Italy?"

"Well, yeah, but why doesn't Charlie just get his car fixed here?" she asked. "Wouldn't it be a lot cheaper?"

"The car's a classic," he explained. "Charlie will only let a bona fide *Italian* Fiat mechanic touch it, and the closest one he could find was in Milan. What are you worried about? Traveling with Charlie will be like traveling with

Grandma. However, I can't say the same for Italian men. Better stay close to Charlie; otherwise they'll be sticking their fingers up every crack you have."

"That's gross"

"You'll see. By the way, a postcard came for you today. From the Netherlands. Gee, I wonder who's in the Netherlands."

Riley had been trying not to think about the young man she'd met her on first day in Europe. His warmth and the funny way he seemed to be able to read her thoughts were quickly pooh-poohed as the result of jet lag. To him, she was a country bumpkin, a girl who dressed in hippie garb, her long blonde hair a perpetual mass of tangles. But still she found herself pouring over maps of the Netherlands, wondering where he might be or what he might be doing. Something important no doubt while she was lunching with Nazis.

"Read it to me," she said as they turned onto the road to Gunthersblum.

"*I miss your smoking hot bod.*"

"Oh he did not write that, Uncle Bob!"

"No. No, you're right. Let me see, what did lover boy say. *Hope things are going well for you. Hope to see you soon. Your tour guide, Gil.* Sheesh, what a romantic! How does he expect to get in your pants with that line!"

Your tour guide. Yup, that just about said it all. What a fool she'd been, imagining, well, all sorts of things she shouldn't have. Fantasizing about a man who thought of her as a dimwitted newbie in a jaded, cynical world who, because of his gallant nature, he had to look after.

"You're crazy, Uncle Bob. That guy thinks of me as a

little sister, his very silly and stupid little sister."

"Right. I always send postcards to women I'm not interested in screwing!"

CHAPTER 13

LATIN LOVERS

CHARLIE NEWSOME ARRIVED at the Worms train station dressed for first-class travel, while Riley, clad in bell bottoms and an oversized sweatshirt, clearly belonged in steerage. Still, he uttered no complaint as they climbed aboard the train to Milan. It was late afternoon on a Friday and the train was already filled to overflowing. Thus they had to push their way past cardboard boxes and well-worn suitcases secured with jute, whose owners lined the narrow corridors.

"Italians, on their way home from the factories for the winter," Charlie explained as he stepped over a box being guarded by a woman slicing a white skinned loaf of salami. She had a face like an apple doll and her head was covered by a magenta scarf tied securely under her chin. "After the war, Germany was a bit short on man power, as you can imagine and so they lured people from Italy and Greece to work at the factories. Only they can't get them to stay through a German winter. Understandably! Most of them are traveling third class, meaning that if second class is full, they have to ride in the halls."

"Swine!" The woman hissed, pointing the knife in his direction as if she'd understood exactly what he'd said.

"*Pardonez,* Senora."

"Swine!" She spat again, mumbling a curse under her breath as she handed slices of salami to the men with her.

Riley followed Charlie closely as they pushed their way through not one, but two packed cars until finally arriving at their private cabin. Only it was already occupied. Occupied by three young men comfortably ensconced amidst their belongings who looked up briefly and then continued with their animated discussion.

Charlie waved his tickets in the air as if they were magic wands. We have this cabin reserved, he attempted to explain in Italian.

There was nary a glance in his direction.

He tried again, this time using a bit more forceful language.

Again, they ignored him.

"Stay here and watch my bag while I find the conductor," Charlie said. They were three and he was just one. Nor were any of the people forced to travel third class likely to aid an American traveling first class.

After he left, Riley stood over his small suitcase and, remembering her uncle's warning, wedged her backside against the door jam. The front of her body she shielded with her backpack.

The young Italians began slowly eyeballing their prey. Up and down, head to toe, again and again while shrugging their shoulders as if thinking why not take a bite? Who would stop us?And then they pounced.

"You American *girla*?"

"Yes."

"*Iya* love *youah*. *Youah* marry me? " They each asked as

they surrounded her.

"Ah..."

"No, no, no! *Iya* love *youah, youah* marry me? Me *Latin lover,* no?"

When she said nothing in return, they resorted to pelvic thrusts to get their point across and twirled their fingers through her hair, chanting, *"Nica, blonda."* The older women made faces and grumbled under their breath while their male counterparts laughed hardily.

"No *comprendez!"* Riley said pushing their hands away ... which only provoked more laughter.

"Nica blonda! You a sexy girla? You wanna marry?"

"No comprendez! Leave me alone!"

She began to think the train had been commandeered by irate seasonal workers who'd locked the conductors in the bathrooms and had perhaps thrown Charlie Newsome overboard. Where was he? Why was he taking so long? And then she heard the sharp slap of a whistle. The first did no good but a second, even sharper slap of the whistle halted what had become lively entertainment at Riley's expense. The crowds parted as the conductor shoved his way through with Charlie following behind.

"What does this mean? Do you all want to be thrown out at the next stop!?" The conductor asked in German. The crowd simmered like a pot of boiling water set to low. Then he turned to the men who'd hijacked a private cabin and ordered them to pick up their boxes and follow him. The young Italians growled like angry puppies and then did as ordered.

As they skulked away one of them whispered something in Charlie's ear. He replied, *"Mi spousa"* putting his arm around Riley's shoulders and pulling her close to his side. The latin lovers kissed the tips of their fingers, and saluted Charlie.

After they left she asked Charlie what they had said.

"They wanted to know how much I wanted for you for the night and I told them you were my wife."

"Couldn't you just have said I was your daughter?"

"That wouldn't have stopped them, my dear. However, a married woman is generally off-limits to an Italian. Just to be safe, tonight I think you'd better limit your journeys to down the hall to the facilities."

Luckily she had a strong bladder.

CHAPTER 14

UNDERWEAR OPTIONAL

"THEY DON'T WEAR UNDERPANTS," Charlie said as he lit another unfiltered cigarette. He and Riley had arrived in Milan at the break of day and quickly grabbed a taxi to the center of town to have breakfast. There were small cafes inside Milano Centrale Statione where they could have had breakfast but Charlie hated Milano Centrale Statione. It was vulgar and pretentious and had been built by that fascist Mussolini. He couldn't wait to get away from its soaring ceilings and twenty foot gods in base relief.

As Riley dug into a plate of spaghetti topped with tons of freshly grated parmesan cheese, Charlie eyeballed the fashionable signorinas strutting past their table while inhaling cigarette after cigarette.

"What?" Riley asked, certain she'd heard him wong.

"They don't wear deodorant or shave either. But they're delicious when they're young, don't you think? They don't always stay that way."

"I have no opinion about Italian women. Why don't you eat your food?"

"I'm not hungry."

"I'm always hungry!"

"Yes, I can see that. And that's delightful, darling, really. But I'm never hungry."

"After breakfast I thought we'd wander around the fashion district before picking up the Fiat. Woman always like to shop."

"That's not true besides..." A middle aged lady in high heels and a leather miniskirt walked past their table carrying several bags with designer labels. "Look at that woman. She's way too old to wear a miniskirt and what's that around her neck?"

"Looks like a fox tail."

"How disgusting!"

Charlie threw up his hands. "Well, then I'm at a loss as to how to entertain you."

"It's alright. It'll be fun to see all the crazy fashions. Maybe I can afford to buy a postcard."

"A postcard?"

"It's probably the only thing I can afford," she said and she was right.

* * *

The train had passed through Switzerland on a cloudy night, thus, there'd been little to see out the window, only the blur of lights as they'd whizzed through town after town without slowing down. Charlie'd watched her curiously for a while and then his eyes closed and his head slipped against the window. For the rest of the night he lay like a broken doll in that position. At one time, he'd probably been a handsome young man, she thought, like Gregory Peck, tall and dark with prominent features and soft eyes. Before the alcohol and cigarettes had taken their toll. Now he looked beyond repair.

Outside their cabin, the Italians'd partied all night

long, laughing and sometimes arguing..Loudly and without any care for first class passengers who might want some shut eye. They were going home for the winter where presumably they'd have plenty of time to sleep. Riley didn't know what awaited her except a long drive home through Switzerland to Germany with the dreariest man on the planet.

CHAPTER 15

ASSASSINARE

THE TAXI DROPPED them off twenty minutes south of downtown Milan in an area of shuttered factories and warehouses.

"This is the Fiat factory?" Riley asked as they approached a flat topped building surrounded by a chain linked fence and topped with barbed wire.

"No. This is where they fix the cars. Wait here," Charlie ordered. He pointed to a concrete bench just outside the gate. "They're not used to women in the shop. I won't be long."

"They're not used to women?"

"Well, not where they work. I won't be long."

She sat on the bench and immediately wished she had a magazine or something to concentrate on instead of her surrounding. Across the street, a row of dead rabbits hung upside down outside a shop whose sign read *Assassinare*, their dark eyes still frozen by fear as blood dripped from their bodies onto the sidewalk. The butcher sauntered out of the shop and strung up another rabbit, wiping his hands on a blood stained apron after the deed was done. Then he pulled a pipe out of his apron pocket and lit it with a match.

He cackled when he spotted Riley across the street her mouth agape. "Caio!" he shouted, pulling one of the rabbits off a hook and wiggling its limp body at Riley. "Bellissimo, si?" Still laughing, he sauntered back into his shop. A few minutes later, a woman cycled up to the row of dead rabbits. She parked her bike and began poking the bodies to make sure they were fresh. Then she turned one over to examine its belly. "Pronto," she yelled and the butcher reemerged. They went down the line, gesturing at each other over costs, and then she paid him, grabbed the bunny she'd chosen, and slung it into the basket on her bike.

That does it. I'm going to become a vegetarian, Riley vowed just as Charlie pulled up to the curb in a deep green sports car with its top down.

"Wow."

"Here's my baby. A 1959 250 Cabriolet from the Pinin Farina era. Only three hundred made!" He claimed, fingering the mahogany and brass steering wheel, "Oh baby, I'm so happy to get you back. Throw the bags in the back, Riley, and let's get out of here."

"Aye, aye, Captain!"

CHAPTER 16

FIRE UNDER THE MOUNTAIN

"I HAVE TO MAKE a quick phone call," Charlie said as he pulled up to a store on the Swiss border. "When I get back, why don't you drive?"

"You're kidding!"

"Once we hit Germany, you'll have to drive. I'm not giving the polizei an excuse to impound this baby! You might as well get some practice before we hit the auto-bahn. I'll get something you to eat too."

"Well …"

"I thought you might be hungry. It's been three hours since your last feeding."

"Ha, ha!"

After he left, Riley slid behind the steering wheel and began to imagine how wonderful it was going to be to drive a classic sports car—with the top down!—through the Swiss Alps. The storm that had passed through the night before left the air clear and crisp and the skies bright blue. For hours they'd seen the mountains looming before them, magical and more majestic than the Sierra Nevada range near her home. And now they were about to enter that magical realm.

In the rearview mirror she could see Charlie in the

phone booth next to the store. On and on he talked as she waited. Finally he disappeared inside the store.

He chuckled when upon returning he found her like a child fingering the switches and gears. "She's a beauty isn't she? More faithful than any of my wives." He threw the keys into her lap and climbed into the passenger seat. The keys were attached to a silver cylinder about the length of her little finger.

"What's this?"

"Oh. That keychain was given to me by one of the exes. I think the cylinder contains a lock of her hair." He reached behind the driver's seat and grabbed a metal flask. Then they were off.

This must be a dream, she thought as they drove into the heart of Switzerland. Anything so beautiful as Switzerland could not be real. Deep valleys in the shadow of snow-topped peaks, serpentine lakes as calm as glass, and villages, so clean, so fresh, so full of health and happiness. Wow, she kept saying. Wow.

Instead of a dream, Charlie Newsome seemed trapped in a nightmare, smoking cigarette after cigarette while drinking from his flask.

"How many times have you been married?" She finally asked.

"Oh, too many times, unfortunately. Yes, indeed. Too many times but would I have done anything differently? Behaved better? I doubt it," he mused. "You know, my second wife was a Parisian model. She was beautiful and had exquisite taste. Ah yes. Exquisite! But so spoiled! Every morning she had to have strawberries and champagne, every morning, every bloody morning. Even in the winter! Let me tell you, it wasn't easy to find fresh strawberries in the winter, especially after the war, but she must have her strawberries so off I would go to find them, fool that I was." He paused, took a long drag, then a sip from his flask. "And chocolates. Oh yes, she must also have *le chocolat*. How she would carry on if I forgot her *chocolat*! *Mon cheri, ou est mon chocolat?* And so of course, I never forgot. Chalene's *chocolat*!"

"Didn't this Chalene get awfully fat, sitting around drinking champagne and eating chocolate all day?"

"Oh no, no. She was so beautiful. She never gained weight."

"How disgusting!"

He laughed, a genuine laugh this time and not his usual snicker. "I ruined my relationship with my daughter over that woman. And the sad part is, if I had it to do over, I probably would do the same damn thing."

Riley had no answer, no apology, no words of comfort. He'd ruined his relationship with his daughter, and yet he freely admitted that he'd go back and do it all over again. And for what? Some idiotic woman who expected soldiers to cater to her every whim while people were starving, a woman who didn't care that he was married, that he had a child. A monster who cared only about herself and yet, he'd gladly…it didn't make any sense. Men were nuts.

They drove the next hour in silence, Charlie drinking from his flask or smoking his cigarette, quietly stewing about something until, unable to control herself, Riley blurted out, "Oh my God. There's no litter in Switzerland!

No Kmarts. No truck stops. It so beautiful here, don't you think?"

"The Swiss are a bunch of bloody hypocrites. Hardly any better than the Nazis."

"What?"

"Goddamned Swiss with their neutrality."

"Maybe they just didn't believe in war."

"Who believes in war? Hell. They stayed neutral because they wanted the money. They wanted to rob from the dead, profit off—" he noticed something by the side of the road. "Hey, slow down. This is our turnoff!"

"You could have warned me!" She said as she veered off the highway and onto a country road. "Where are we going now?".

"We're taking the train through that mountain," Charlie said.

"That mountain?" The mountain in front of them spanned the horizon.

"Yup. Are you ready?"

"I dunno. How long does it take?"

"Oh, about an hour. But our alternative is to go over Gotthard Pass which would take us a lot longer, if the pass is open, which it almost never is."

"An hour in a dark tunnel? It doesn't sound safe."

"You can't beat Swiss engineering. They might be goddamned bastards with no heart, but they're damn good engineers. Besides the road over the summit is a killer, especially in a vintage car. Storms can come creeping up on you at any time and—"

"Okay, okay. The tunnel it is."

An hour, Riley thought as Charlie pulled the canvas roof over the top of the car. "It won't do much good but it's better than nothing." An hour sitting in the Fiat on a flat bed train car with nothing to look at but the walls of tunnel. Nothing to listen to but the clackety-clack of the train as it rolled along.

"What do you mean?"

"You'll see. Damned convenient, the train, but they've got to fix the ventilation system. Maybe we'll get some entertainment."

"Some trolls or dwarves—"

"I was thinking along the x-rated line." Charlie grabbed the bag from the backseat and pulled forth a loaf of bread and chunk of cheese. "Lunch and a movie. I believe we've gotten lucky."

"What are you talking about?"

"The Citroën, of course."

The tunnel was lit by long rectangular panels spaced such that every couple of seconds they got a quick glimpse of the people in the car in front of them. There appeared to be four people, two in front and two in the back. First they began pecking at each other like nervous chickens and then…

"Are they taking off their clothes?"

"Bien sur! An X-rated romance!" Charlie confirmed, as minutes later the tiny car began rocking back and forth.

"Oh, gross." Riley groaned as the lovemaking went on and on and on. Fifteen, twenty minutes until finally the car stopped rocking and smoke rose from all four windows.

"Smoke break,"Charlie said as he also lit a cigarette. "It can't be over so soon. They must be Germans! Boo, hiss! Let's demand a refund."

"I need a cigarette. Give me a cigarette, Charlie."

He just snickered.

"I mean it!"

"I'm not bringing you back to your uncle's with a smoke hanging out of your mouth."

"He wouldn't care."

A naked man emerged from the front seat of Citroën and climbed into the back.

"Look, Riley. It was only an intermission. Now comes the good stuff—a ménage à trois. They must be French!"

Soon the car began rocking once again. This time they didn't stop until the proverbial light at the end of the tunnel appeared.

"Gawd. What's wrong with those people?"

"It happens all the time. What else are you going to do for an hour sitting on a car train?"

"Isn't it illegal?"

"Ha!"

CHAPTER 17

THE HAPPY LAND OF THE SWISS

THEIR PLANS HAD BEEN to spend the night in Bern but by the time they reached the turnoff, Charlie had changed his mind. "I'm not in the mood for German food. It's so bland. Beefsteak in gravy. Ugh. Let's spend the night in Neuchâtel, instead. I know a great place, with absolutely fabulous French food. And it's not that far out of our way."

"Do they have fondue?"

"Of course."

"And hot chocolate? Real Swiss hot chocolate?"

"Of course," he laughed. "You know, I can't say you're the most beautiful girl I've ever met, but there is something about you that's intriguing."

"That I like to eat?"

"No, no. Just something."

No girl likes to be told she's not the most beautiful thing on the planet, Riley thought. No wonder his love life had been such a mess. He was too darn honest.

* * *

Charlie's great place turned out to be a three-story hunting lodge on the shores of Lake Neuchâtel, a long, narrow body of water lying at the foot of the relatively gentle Jura Range. As they parked the car, he explained how the villages in the Jura were famous for fine watch-making. Not damned cuckoo clocks, mind you, but fine watches, like Movados. Thousand dollar masterpieces of Swiss engineering. They'd arrived just as the sun was setting, taking every bit of warmth with it. Riley was anxious to get inside but Charlie dawdled, rising ever slowly from the Fiat, stretching his legs and smoothing back his hair. He sighed as he gazed out at the lake as though seeing it for the first time.

"Come on Charlie, I'm cold. Let's go in!"

"We used to come here every summer. Escape the heat of Paris for a month and...Look, isn't this beautiful?" He took a few steps towards the lake and then noticing that she wasn't following, he turned around. "Oh, I'm sorry dear. You do look chilled. I can do my reminiscing from the warmth of the lodge."

The proprietress greeted them at the door as if their arrival had been expected and not Charlie's last minute whim. This is Madame Blanc, he explained, an old friend of mine. She was a tiny woman, barely five feet tall, with grey-blond hair pulled back into a tight French roll. She wore little makeup but her eyebrows had been trained into a permanent arch of surprise and waxed dark brown, and the skin on her face had been ironed free of wrinkles, an effort, no doubt, to look younger which only emphasized the dullness of her eyes. They were soon deep in conversation as Riley fidgeted. She was glad that grumpy old Charlie still had someone in his life who could make him laugh but too tired to politely stand around while they yammered at each other in French.

"Pardonez, I really need to take a bath."

Madame Blanc seemed startled by Riley's rudeness. "Bien sur," she said, handing her a key. "Your rooms are on the third floor. We dine at eight."

Riley had been looking forward to a lake view but instead her room faced the pastures behind the lodge where black and white cows shuffled towards the evening trough, their cow bells tinkling. It was such a peaceful scene … just as she'd always imagined Switzerland that her disappointment soon faded. She drew a bath, and slid into the hot soapy water, mentally composing the letters she would send home. *Switzerland is everything I imagined it to be: peaceful, clean and so safe. I feel like I'm in heaven.*

Around six o'clock she grew tired of writing letters full of hyperbole and decided to retrieve the remnants of their lunch from the Fiat. There were only a few scraps of bread but it would hold her until that ungodly hour when the hotel's dining room finally opened. Eight o'clock what a horrible time to have dinner. She was certain that was one European tradition she'd never get used to. But once she got to the front porch of the lodge she stopped. Charlie was standing under the one lamppost struggling to pull a tarp over the Fiat in a stiff breeze. He looks so silly, she thought, tucking in his precious car for the night. Silly but sweet. She thought about the strawberries in the winter, the champagne every morning. Perhaps he was too much of a romantic.

She started toward the Fiat but stopped when she heard Charlie's voice rise in anger. "Trop tard," he kept saying to someone standing in the mist off the lake. A figure with hands in the pockets of a grey overcoat neither moving nor speaking.

Instinctively she returned to the lobby and feigned interest in the many animal heads mounted on the walls.

"Is the car okay?" She asked when Charlie finally came inside.

"She's set for the night. Hey, I bet you're hungry," he said. "Americans can't stand eating late. My fourth wife was an American, you know. Round about the time I finally got her used to late suppers, she decided she didn't like me enough to hang around for the pension." He laughed as if it were a joke.

"That's terrible."

"No it's not. The fifth had a far better sense of humor. I'll get you a couple of breadsticks so you don't die of hunger."

* * *

It was a quiet night for the lodge. Besides Charlie and the young woman, there was a French family with two inordinately well-behaved little girls and a hunter sitting quietly by himself. The menu was fixed: fondue or mountain trout. Riley ordered the fondue, Charlie the fish. She dug right in. Charlie picked.

"You know," he began. "I just had a thought. Ariel and

I—Ari was my first wife—used to take the back road from Paris to this lodge every damn summer and it was jolly good fun. It starts just down the road from here and then forks at La-Chaux-de-Fonds, with one branch heading north towards her parents' house in Nancy and the other west towards Paris. It's quite lovely and should still be open. Of course, you wouldn't want to take it if you have a heart condition!" He laughed as he picked at the fish, separating bones from flesh, peppering it until it was almost black. "Somewhere along the route, I can't really remember where, there's a one-lane tunnel manned at both ends by two old varmints. The "Billy Goats Gruff," I used to call them. Do you remember that story?"

"Of course!"

"Any way these two old geezers had quite a gig going. You paid one of them to enter and the other to exit! Ha! Our daughter, Sophie, she was scared to death of them."

"Maybe we should take that route home?"

Charlie laughed and then took a long drag on his cigarette. "I'm tempted but, nah. Raferman would kill me. I promised to bring him back a case of some overrated Italian liquor I had the mechanics pick up for me. It's in the trunk. If anything happens to me, you'd better make sure to get it to him. He's got some big shindig coming up and he's very serious about his shindigs."

"Why is everyone afraid of Lou Raferman?"

Charlie laughed. "He's just not a good man to underestimate, that's all. I think he'd be flattered if he thought

97

people were afraid of him."

"Is Sophie the daughter…?"

"The one I screwed up? Yeah, you can say it. Just say it. I screwed it up. Some things, once they get broken, you can never put them back together," he sighed, smothering his cigarette in what was left of his mashed potatoes. He turned his head towards Madame Blanc and lifted his glass. "Un autre!"

"I don't believe that's true."

"I'm living proof that it is."

Madame Blanc responded to Charlie's request by putting an entire bottle of cognac on the table. Then she sat down to share it with him. Riley figured that was her cue to leave. "Don't open the door to anyone tonight," Charlie said as she made her exit. "Switzerland is not as safe and wonderful as they'd like you to believe."

CHAPTER 18

THE CONFESSION

RILEY FELL ASLEEP fantasizing about her first morning in Switzerland. It would include, of course, creamy hot chocolate and a freshly baked croissant delivered to her as she lounged in bed under the warm comforter. Later she would meet Charlie in the lobby and they would continue their drive, stopping for a lunch next to an Alpine lake where swans floated peacefully and flowers bloomed profusely. A day to remember forever before returning to Germany.

Instead she awoke to sirens, at first in the distance and then growing louder and louder until she realized they were beneath her window. Car doors slammed. Footsteps echoed down the hall. Thinking the place was on fire, she leapt from bed, threw a blanket over her shoulders and ran to the window. Two police cars and an ambulance were at the back of the lodge, no fire trucks. Someone had an accident was her next thought. Maybe someone working in the kitchen for that dreadful Madame Blanc.

She was about to get dressed and venture out to see what was going on when there was a knock at the door.

"Who is it?"

"Mademoiselle O'Tannen?" It was Madame Blanc.

"Oui."

"Mademoiselle, c'est le polezei."

She opened the door a crack. Behind Madame Blanc stood a stocky, balding man with a grim, humorless face.

"You must come with me," he said. "Vous comprendez?"

"No. I do not comprendez."

"You are traveling with Monsieur Newsome, no?"

"Yes. What's going on?"

"He is dead."

"That can't be." She looked past the policeman and down the hall to the room at end. Charlie's room. The door was wide open and there was a lump under a white sheet on the floor. "Oh my God!"

"Please, mademoiselle, go with *le constable*," Madame Blanc said. "He has questions."

"But why can't he question me here?"

"S'il vous plaît, mademoiselle. I must type a report. It is just, as you say, a routine."

"Can I get dressed?"

"Oui."

Riley dressed and did as ordered.

* * *

"So you are the niece of the late Monsieur Newsome?" The constable asked, as he struggled to insert a triple-carbon form into his typewriter. His windowless office was a few miles down the road from the hotel.

When she didn't respond immediately, he looked up from his typewriter and glared at her.

"I'm not his niece! I didn't even know him that well."

"Please tell me, why did Monsieur Newsome tell Madame Blanc that you were his niece if you were not his niece?"

"I don't know."

"Are you his mistress?"

"Of course I wasn't his mistress. He was old enough to be my father!"

"How long have you been in Switzerland?"

"A day."

"Why were you here?"

"We're just driving through from Milan."

"Why did you stay the night in Neuchâtel? It is out of your way."

"Because we wanted to have fondue. Listen. Why are you asking all these questions? Shouldn't I be allowed to call my uncle? Or the American embassy?"

Le constable rolled his eyes. "Let us get to, as you say, the punch line. Do you work for the CIA like Monsieur Newsome, mademoiselle?"

"What?"

"Of course, you would not tell me."

"That's just crazy! I'm a hippie! Charlie Newsome was just a sad, sad man who'd been married too many times! He works for the Department of the Army, not the CIA, for crying out loud."

The constable ignored her. He pulled his report from the typewriter and handed her the pile. "Sign here," he ordered, indicating a line on the top sheet.

"I can't sign something I don't understand. This is all in French!"

"You must! It is only answers to questions which *you* give me!"

"I have to contact my uncle. My *real* uncle."

"You can call your uncle at the hotel. You must stay a few days in hotel. You must not leave."

"No way! I don't have any money! And I'm not signing a statement that's in French."

Le constable sprang to his feet. My God, he's going to strangle me, Riley thought. Instead he reached into a cabinet behind him and pulled a pile of Swiss francs from a tin box. This would hold you over at the hotel, he explained, until the investigation is over.

"Sign the statement and Hans will drive you back to the hotel."

"No, I won't sign!"

The constable's face went blank. "What? You will not sign?"

"That's right."

He began pacing the floor.

"I'm sure Charlie died of a heart attack or stroke. He smoked like a furnace and drank all day long."

"You are not suspect of a crime! This is just what you say. I will have it translated and brought to the hotel. Then you sign," he announced, waving to his driver. "Prendre son retour à l'hôtel," which Riley imagined translated into "Get this idiot out of my sight!"

Madame Blanc greeted her at the front door of the lodge. She'd pulled herself together since the early morning, fresh powder covered her cheeks and her blonde-grey hair was molded into that tight French roll again. It had been a *horrible, horrible* morning, she whined, but now it was time to move on. She had a business to run and new guests arriving soon. "You will perhaps stay in your room and I will have—"

"Did you reach my uncle?"

"No one is at the number you give me. But I have called to Monsieur Raferman and left him a massage."

"Message. You know Lou Raferman?"

"*Mais oui.* Many years now. If you need anything remember, please to stay in your room and I will have delivered. You must not speak to anyone of what has happen."

CHAPTER 19

NO ONE TO CALL

AFTER SHE RETURNED TO HER ROOM Riley locked the door. Then she climbed under the thick featherbed to try to get warm. She kept imagining the morgue where Charlie now lay naked on a stainless steel gurney alongside other cold, lifeless bodies. And she was there with him naked and frozen. Unable to get warm no matter how many pots of hot chocolate Madame Blanc had sent up.

Every now and then she heard footsteps in the hall. Sometimes they stopped just outside her door and she heard heavy breathing. At first she hoped it was Charlie. That he wasn't really dead and she was just waking up from a terrible nightmare. Soon there would be a knock. A knock and then his voice: "Are you ready to go yet? Hurry up, it's a beautiful morning; we'll take the back road, past the Billie Goats Gruff! We'll have lunch in an Alpine meadow and watch the cows graze."

But there was no knock and the footsteps continued down the hall. Once she opened the door just a sliver and peeked out. Three men in dark suits gathered around the spot where Charlie's body had once lain, speaking in low voices and taking notes. She watched as they searched the room, opening the drawers and pulling clothes from his small suitcase. What could they possibly be looking for?

And then it dawned on her. Maybe he hadn't had a heart attack. Maybe he really was with the CIA and someone had killed him, like Madame Blanc, or maybe the man she'd heard him arguing with in the parking lot the night before. The whole story of picking up a vintage car might have been a cover-up for something much more clandestine.

She picked up the phone and demanded that Madame Blanc put her through to uncle's house. The phone rang and rang and rang. Eventually Madame Blanc came back on the line asking if she wanted to call someone else. She thought of calling her parents and waking them in the middle of the night. *Hello, it's your daughter. I just got back from the police station because Uncle Bob sent me to Italy with his friend who then went and died and the police think I was the dead man's mistress and that he was a CIA spy ... so come over and save me.* Oh yeah. That would work. They'd probably think I was high on pot and hang up on me.

No, Madame Blanc, I have no one else to call.

She could hear the tinkling of the cows' bells as they trod slowly up the hill. Such an ordinary day for them. The sun shown down and breezes blew gently with just a whisper of the coming winter. *Ah, to be a Swiss dairy cow, without a care in the world.* She heard a maid running a vacuum cleaner in the hall and watched a delivery truck unload boxes at the back door. Just an ordinary day for them.

After about an hour of routine morning activity suddenly the lodge became eerily quiet. She couldn't hear the cows or even the birds singing. The cars and trucks parked behind the lodge had all disappeared. She called the front desk only to get the answering machine. She left her room and went in search of some sign of life. All three floors were quiet and empty, even the kitchen. She pictured her own head hanging on the wall between the elk and bearded goat. "Forget staying here," she said aloud "I've seen this movie before!"

CHAPTER 20

THE DEAD RIDE ALONG

THE TARP HAD BEEN RIPPED from the Fiat and thrown into the bushes; the trunk was open and empty, but no one was in the parking lot and no one was watching from the hotel. Riley closed the trunk and climbed behind the wheel. The Swiss police had no right to make her stay—it had to be against the Geneva Convention or something. She had no friend, no one to stand up for her, and she wasn't about to sign a form she couldn't understand. For all she knew, it was a confession of guilt, an admission that she was some sort of CIA spy. Not to mention the fact that something quite odd was going on in that lodge. It had been abandoned which only meant one thing. Something bad was going to happen and they wanted no witnesses.

Charlie'd said that the road to La-Chaux-de-Fonds was easy to find and he was right. In fact it was so easy to find that she began to doubt her luck. Whenever a road started out that smoothly in her life, it meant trouble ahead. Still, when the police realized she had gone, they'd probably check the main roads and not some little known backroad to France.

* * *

"You were right," Riley told the man who'd slipped into the passenger seat beside her as they drove along. "It is a magical drive. I feel like I'm in the Sound of Music. But I haven't run into any tunnels guarded by the Billie Goats Gruff yet. Did you make up that story up to frighten me as you had your daughter? You did, didn't you?"

It wasn't a surprise that suddenly he was there. She knew Charlie would never abandon his one true love! His body, yes, but his car, never. Nor would he miss out a drive so filled with memories of happier times. "But you know, this road isn't so bad! It's not nearly as steep or deadly as Donner Pass. But then you always did drive like a little old lady."

He took umbrage with a chuckle. His spirit seem so light, so different high in those gentle hills. So happy. His chuckle rose into the sky as a playful cloud.

They reached La-Chaux-de-Fonds around noon. "Which way next?" Riley asked. She faced a pole with road signs pointing in all directions, none of which read "This way to Paris" or "This way to Germany. Instead they pointed to places like Baume-les-Dames, or Montbéliard.

But Charlie had vanished. She was alone.

So she took the money the constable had given her and bought a map of France and a bottle of Orangina. Then she sat by the side of the road and plotted a route that, at least on paper, would lead her to Sarreguemines where she and her uncle had had lunch only a week before. From there she was confident she could find her way to Worms.

However Riley did not know that in rural France you have to plot your journey on the microscopic level, from hole in the wall to hole in the wall. It's not enough to know your final destination or the next big city on your route. You have to know the name of the next village because your choice when you get to a crossroads isn't Paris or Sarreguemines; it's Saint Germain des Hundes or Grandcamp-Maisy—some five-cottage kink in the road that leads to another five-cottage kink in the road. Choose the wrong kink and you could easily find yourself miles off track with no way to get back on track, except to reverse your route. Which is exactly what happened to Riley. Many times. Thus, several hours later, she arrived in Gunthersblum a wreck, both emotionally and physically. She'd spent the day circling in roundabouts, forced to retrace her route all while crying out in frustration and damning herself for not staying in Neuchâtel. How stupid she'd been for overreacting. How immature.

She found her uncle sitting on the recliner with a glass of bourbon in his hand, the fat yellow cat on his lap. "It's about time you got home," he said, not even turning to glance in her direction. "Now that I don't have to wake my sister up with the grim news that you've disappeared, I think I'll head up to bed."

Riley dropped her backpack on the floor in disgust.

That's all he had to say? "Charlie Newsome died last night, Uncle Bob!"

"So I've heard. Heart attack. Won't know for sure until the autopsy, but that would be my guess."

"They, the Swiss police I mean, expected me to stay in Switzerland and sign some form."

"Then why didn't you?"

"They wanted me to sign a document that was in French, Uncle Bob! I have no idea what it said. And not only that, they thought Charlie and I were CIA spies!"

"Well, are you?"

"Ha, ha. By the way, I'm starving."

"There are crackers and peanut butter in the kitchen."

He dislodged the cat by standing up. "It's been a long day. We'll sort everything out tomorrow."

"But don't you want to hear my story."

"In the morning, Niecey. It's been a long day."

The day, which had begun in a hotel room in Switzerland, dreaming of hot chocolate and flakey, buttery croissants, ended in Germany with peanut butter and Saltine crackers. But, her uncle fell to sleep so peacefully in his spartan bedroom, so unconcerned about everything that Riley began to believe her nightmare was over.

As usual, she was wrong.

CHAPTER 21

OMIE HAS A TALE TO TELL

"I'M MAKING EGGS WITH HATS. How many would you like?"

"Just one." It was still dark outside but her uncle's off key singing had made it impossible to get back to sleep. "What time is it?"

"The sun will be up soon...Just one?" On the counter lay several slices of white bread. Oil was already sizzling in the skillet.

"Okay, two."

"I thought we'd have time to talk about your little adventure this morning," he said, punching a hole in each piece of bread with an overturned juice glass, "but we won't."

"What?"

"You're going to Paris." He calmly retrieved an egg carton from the fridge.

"Why?"

He started singing in response to her question: *"When Johnny comes marching home again—hurrah! hurrah! We'll give a hardy welcome in—hurrah! hurrah!"*

"Uncle Bob, have you lost your mind? I feel like I'm in a Fellini movie."

"Oh we'll all feel gay when Johnny comes marching home!"

Outside the quiet of the morning was broken by a rumbling sound. Uncle Bob dropped the bread slices into the sizzling grease and began cracking eggs. "You better eat fast," he said, "then pack a few things."

A moving van with no markings whatsoever ground to a stop in front of the house. As it did, a light flickered on across the street. The old woman who lived in the house, the old woman they called Omie, peered out from behind lace curtains as the van pulled into her driveway and then, seconds later, roughly reversed gears and backed up into Uncle Bob's driveway. When it reached Charlie's Fiat, the rear gate flew open and several men in camouflage jumped out.

"Oh my God," Riley said, as they proceeded to lower a ramp. "It's the Swiss Police."

"Relax, it's just Lou Raferman's crew."

"What are they going to do?"

"Watch and see," he replied, not even turning in the direction of the window as he flipped a couple of eggs with hats onto a plate and set it on the table. "Eat. It may be your last chance for a while."

In less than five minutes the men attached chains to the Fiat's bumper, cranked it up the ramp into the back of the truck, slammed the doors shut, and left.

"Why did they—" The phone in the hall rang.

"I'll take the call upstairs. Don't wait for me. Eat."

They tasted good, those eggs with hats. She ate like a truck driver, even soaking up the runny yolks with the crispier edges of deep fried bread. Real protein. And real orange juice, not that orange-colored water. But it was hell waiting for her uncle to return. What had he meant?

Overnight the weather had changed. As the sky grew lighter, children rode past the house on their way to school, bundled against the cold in such a way that only their red cheeks and noses were visible. In the distance, the always-on-time train hooted through the river valley. Omie emerged to sweep her front porch, a scarf sharply tied under her chin and thick black galoshes on her tiny feet. The concrete porch wasn't particularly dirty, but it was her habit to sweep it every morning. As she did, she took clandestine glances across the street. Riley figured she would be over later to ask "Oncle Boob" (as the villagers now called him) why an unmarked moving van full of soldiers had backed up into his driveway early in the morning and disappeared with a fancy sports car. She spoke no English and he, little German, so the story circulated through town would probably contain more conjecture than fact.

After a while Riley gave up waiting for her uncle to return. She washed off her dish and went upstairs to take a bath, after which she dressed and returned downstairs.

"You sure do like to dawdle in that bathtub. Pack a few things," he ordered. "You don't have much time."

"Why?"

"I told you. You're going to Paris. Lou will be here any minute."

"I'm going to Paris with Lou Raferman?"

"Yeah. What are you complaining about, anyway? You'll love Paris, although Lou might live to regret this decision. If he lives. You're not going to kill him off too, are you?"

"That doesn't make any sense. Why don't you just send me back to Switzerland? I'll sign the stupid paper. I promise I won't get freaked out again. I think it was just, you know, the shock of everything."

"Nooooooo. You've done enough. I'm going down to there to handle things. Apparently Charlie didn't have any next of kin that they can find."

"But why did Mr. Raferman have Charlie's car towed off?"

"Beats me, Niecey. It's not like you're on the FBI's Most Wanted List. Just let Lou handle things and don't ask a lot of questions. Now run along and pack."

Despite the overcast skies, Lou Raferman arrived wearing sunglasses, wide-rimmed Jackie O sunglasses. He strode into the kitchen and without saying hello sat down heavily at the table. "Damned shame about Newsome. At least it was a heart attack, quick, no suffering. Despite his problems, damn fine man."

"Yup."

"Oh, hello there young lady," he finally took note of Riley.

"Hello Mr. Raferman."

"Although Charles really did have a talent for making messes. Lord, remember that phony Countess de Longenberry? What an unmitigated disaster! He dies and there's yet another mess."

"What about his…"

"His remains? Robert, I'll let you figure that one out with Veteran's Affairs if we can't find his daughter."

The enormity of the last twenty-four hours chose to hit Riley at that exact moment. A wonderful man had died. A liberator of concentration camps. Why hadn't she been nicer to him instead of always trying to get him to see the world her way? "He was such a wonderful man! Saving all those Jews! And he was so nice to me, but I was so mean to him. I was even mad at him for dying and ruining my trip! I'm so insensitive!" She said, grabbing a napkin from the table and loudly blowing her nose. "I can't believe I was so selfish and thinking only of myself. We have to find Sophie! We just have to and let her know that her father loved her!"

"Hell. He spent his last day on earth traveling through Switzerland with a girl young enough to be his daughter! I can think of worse ways to go," Uncle Bob said reaching into the cabinet for a glass. "Lou, would you like a bourbon?"

"A little early, don't you think Robert? My dear, I assure you we will try to find his daughter."

"Can you imagine liberating those awful camps? Seeing all those atrocities! Bodies piled on top of each other. Children even! And he saved them! Yes, we have to find his daughter! He talked about her. Said he'd screwed everything."

"Ah, err. Should we get you an aspirin or something?"

"I don't understand why I have to go to Paris."

"*Have to go*? I *have to* go to Paris so it seemed logical for you to come with me while your uncle, err, settles things in Switzerland. I live in a very central locale, from which you can walk to many of the famous sites. I cannot think of a better place for you to recoup from your obvious, uh-hem, trauma, can you, Robert?"

"No, Paris will be just the tonic for her."

She hadn't the strength to argue with both men. Maybe they were right. What would she do in Gunthersblum all alone, especially now that the weather had changed? At least in Paris she could go to the Louvre. Yes, and sample French pastries, sip tea at a sidewalk café, stroll along the Seine. "You're right. I can't stay here alone. Thank you Mr. Raferman."

CHAPTER 22

LAPIN AU JUS

SHE AWOKE TO *BLACK IS BLACK,* I *want my baby back.*
Sung in both English and French on the radio. *It's grey, it's*
grey since she went away. At Lou Raferman's insistence
("you look horrible") she'd stretched out on the backseat
of the limo while he rode in front with his driver. *I'm nev-*
er able to nap during the day, she'd insisted but soon after
leaving Worms, the gentle rocking of the car and the rain
hitting the roof lulled her to sleep.

The driver noticed her stirring in the rearview mirror
and mumbled something to his boss. Lou opened the
sliding window between the compartments: "We're on
the outskirts of Paris now, my dear. Perfect time for you
to wake up."

"I never fall asleep in the daytime. I must be coming
down with something."

"No, no, my dear. You've just had a trauma. Perhaps
this will help. Your uncle gave me some letters for you."
He passed through a short stack of mail.

Riley shifted through them rapidly. One was from her
father. Another from her best friend. The third was a
postcard from Gil.

"I got a postcard from Gil. But it doesn't say too
much."

"That's nice, dear," Lou replied, not turning from the stack of papers on his own lap.

"I think he feels protective of me, like I'm his little sister or something."

"Don't ask me to explain that young man, my dear. I'm just his boss and not his romantic advisor. I do hope this weather rolls through so that you can enjoy Paris."

The colors of Paris ran together in the heavy mist, like stained glass windows melting. She thought of her boyfriend back home. He was much too busy to write, too busy with all his various extracurricular activities. He was president of so many clubs and societies that he barely had time to even study. They were so different. He was practical, ambitious, driven and she was a dreamer... They were the perfect pair, she thought as she read Gil's postcard again.

"Did he give you anything to hold onto for him, my dear?"

"What? Gil? No!"

"Oh no, dear. Not Gilbert, but Charles. Did he give you anything? Anything at all?"

"No, of course not."

"Are you sure? Think about it."

She thought a minute and then a light went off. "Oh, I'm sorry, Mr. Raferman, but someone broke into the Fiat's trunk and stole it. I think it was the Swiss Police!"

"Really?"

"Yeah, the trunk was totally empty. I'm sorry about your party."

"What do you mean? What did the police steal?"

"The liquor. It was gone."

Lou looked confused. "Liquor."

"For your party. Charlie got in Milan for you."

"I see. But he did give you anything else? Anything at all, no matter how small?"

"Nope."

"Now think. Anything?"

"Nope, nothing."

The closer they got to the center of Paris the crazier the traffic became. "Why's everyone so angry? I thought this was the city of love?"

"It's the city of romantic love, not brotherly love. Don't worry, my apartment is an oasis of calm."

He was right. It took a long time but eventually they emerged from all the chaos to an area of broad boulevards and neighborhoods where buildings were not built one on top of the other. In contrast to its rugged shell, the core of Paris was calm. Almost too calm. The celestial architecture and monuments, the gentle flow of people walking hand in hand along the Seine—all seemed suspended in time and somewhat unnatural.

"Wow," Riley kept saying as they drove past the Louvre and Notre Dame. Wow, wow, wow. In the drizzle they didn't seem real. Surely she was dreaming. Wow, wow, wow, wow.

Lou's flat on Quai Bourbon wasn't nearly as large as his penthouse in Worms nor as extravagant in decor. In Paris, Lou explained, you're never really home so you don't need a big and fancy place. Just a pied-à-terre (which is what he called his place) will do. The *salon* had high ceilings but was narrow and sparsely furnished. The *salle a manger* (where Riley would sleep) had been converted into a guest room with the addition of a day bed and massive wardrobe. Just inside the front door was a tiny kitchen and closet sized bedroom where Lou's driver, who also served as his "man," slept.

"And now I must work. I will see you around eightish at which time we will join a dear friend of mine for dinner." Lou said as he unlocked the door to his private office and bedroom. "Feel to wander the neighborhood or just relax."

"I feel like I might be coming down with something so I think I'll stay out of the rain and write some letters."

"A woman of letters! Excellent. If you get bored, there are copies of Stars and Stripes in the kitchen. I hear that, like your uncle, you're a puzzle whiz. That ability does run in the DNA. Aziz always has a pot of tea brewing and crumpets, in case you're hungry but please don't overdo. You want to save all your room for dinner!"

You'll never guess where I am now! She wrote to C, who'd married young and now sat tending the two babies that she'd had with a philandering, no-good and worthless husband. *Paris!* She went on to describe the adventures of her short time in Europe, page after page until she started to worry that they might come off as unbelievable. Even if they didn't, C's greatest adventure these days was getting to the grocery store. Somehow it seemed wrong. She ripped up what she'd written and instead described the banality of the officers' club and the hatred Germans seemed to have for Americans, things that wouldn't remind C that she was stuck in a subdivision in the desert with two small children while she sat looking out at the lights of Paris.

Her fingers were about to fall off from writing letters when Lou knocked on the door. It was time to prep for their date. Prep for Riley would be slipping on the one dress she'd brought to Europe. Lou's prep took far longer and so she waited for him in the kitchen completing the puzzle pages, her stomach growling as she imagined all of the French delicacies she would soon be tasting. The quiches, the souffles, and that miracle of all miracles: chocolate mousse!

* * *

Their dinner date was Mrs. Chrisholder, an English-woman visiting Paris with her book club. She was on the verge of middle age but still in good shape (in England we walk every day, she explained). Riley got the feeling that Colonel Chrisholder (one of Lou's war buddies) was an older man because they had no children, but ap-parently, many dogs. The restaurant was below ground on a quiet side street. The interior reminded Riley of a Toulouse Lautrec painting with the heavy velvet curtains and toile wallpaper, a mahogany bar with brass railings, but sans the streetwalkers. Lou had his own *special* table near the casement windows, thus they could watch dogs walk by. Why that was such a plus was a mystery to Ri-ley..

"So, how did you come to know Lou? Are you related," Mrs. Chrisholder whispered as Lou informed the waiter of the wines they'd be having with each course and the brand of champagne for their cheese and fruit. Madame and he might have a cognac afterwards but mademoiselle probably would not.

"No, my uncle works for him. He had to go to Switzerland—"

Lou heard the word Switzerland and switched his attention from the waiter to Mrs. Chrisholder, "You do remember Newsome, the fellow always—and infernally!—falling *madly* in love? Well, he's dead, heart attack, and I had to send Mademoiselle's uncle to Switzerland to take care of the arrangements. We can't find even *one* of them, his *five* wives I mean, or the daughter. Of course we couldn't leave this innocent young lady by herself in Germany. Lord knows what sort of trouble she would have gotten herself into. She seems to have the knack for trouble. I had to come down to Paris anyway so it ..."

"The *knack* for trouble? How intriguing. I do vaguely remember Newsome. A bit young for a heart attack, wasn't he? Well, you never know," she replied. "Are you a hippie, my dear? I do believe there are some in London, none in the country, of course. They seem to prefer the cities, don't they?"

"Uh, well..."

"Don't most young people?" Lou interjected. "Prefer the cities, I mean. I absolutely detested small town life!"

"But all the best murders occur in small villages."

"I'll have to defer to your expertise in that arena, my dear."

Being old acquaintances, they soon began to reminisce about—what else? The War. People who'd died, people who had retired someplace warm, people who'd simply disappeared. The War, the War, the War. It was as if the War had ended only yesterday and not twenty-five years earlier.

Meanwhile Riley guzzled the wine. She hadn't had much experience with alcohol, just champagne at weddings. And her uncle drank only hard liquor which he wasn't going to share with a twenty year old. The white wine that came with the first course (a consommé) was light and sweet and so she had two glasses. The rose colored wine served with fish was also light. "Un autre, s'il vous plaît," became her favorite phrase. The more she drank, the more attractive the waiters became.

After several glasses of wine, she simply had to tell the waiters how wonderful they were. "How do you say 'you are such wonderful waiters'?" She asked Lou.

He turned from his conversation with Mrs. Chrisholder. "How many glasses of wine have you had, my dear?"

"Oh, I dunno. They just keep giving me more."

"Well, perhaps you should pace yourself. The main course is next and it's something you want to save your palate for. People make reservations months in advance just to taste Chef Michel's lapin au jus!"

Lapin, she thought. What the heck was that? Before she had a chance to ask, the main course arrived. The lump of browned meat on her plate slightly resembled a very plump chicken thigh. It was covered with sauce and dressed with grilled celery. "Mr. Raferman, doesn't 'lapin' mean 'rabbit?'"

"No, it means 'Hare,'" he replied rather stiffly.

Riley poked the meat with her fork. It jiggled. Not only did they expect her to eat a bunny, but an underdone bunny. A bunny butchered by some horrible man in a dirty apron, then hung outside a shop to drip blood onto the sidewalk. Once it had had soft fur and a funny little nose. Once it had hopped merrily through fields doing harm to no one. Then it was slaughtered.

"I can't eat this," she said to the waiter. "I'm too full. J'ai trop mangé."

"My dear, it's the chef's signature dish! You must eat it." Lou commanded, "Mangé, mangé!"

"It's a bunny, Mr. Raferman. A bunny!"

"It is a rabbit and you must eat it!"

"I can't." Tears ran down her cheeks and onto the bunny.

The waiter grabbed her plate. "Végétarienne!" he snorted.

Lou's mouth fell open. He glanced towards the kitchen as though at any moment the chef would emerge with a cleaver. Then he stood up, threw money on the table, and announced they were leaving.

CHAPTER 23

THE DEADLY DAMES

THE NEXT MORNING Riley was surprised to be greeted civilly by Lou Raferman. After all she'd *obliterated* his relationship with one of Paris' top chefs...*perhaps forever.* Something she hadn't needed to do. She could have easily pretended to enjoy the Lapin au Jus like a civilized young lady. They'd barely gotten back to his flat when he'd hurried to his office and slammed the door leaving her to wonder how miserable the rest of her trip to Paris would be.

"I'm so sorry about last night," she began, "I should have —"

"Yes, yes and I shouldn't have been so testy! As Bettina rightly pointed out, I should have kept my eye on your wine consumption but I'm not used to chaperoning." He looked up at Riley from his cup of tea. "Well, no excuses. I have some news, my dear."

"Did Uncle Bob call?"

"No. No updates on that score. My news is that Bettina, uh, Mrs. Chrisholder, wants you to accompany her book club on a tour of the Louvre this morning. I'm not sure why after your behavior at Chez Michel last night. Perhaps she's taken pity on me, dear thing. Would you like to go?"

"Of course."

"Excellent. I'll let her know." He looked at his wrist-watch. "They mean to start the tour as soon as the galleries open so you'd best get ready and then I'll have my man walk you over." Lou's 'man' was a dark-skinned Moroccan who spoke French as though on speed and smoked unfiltered cigarettes that smelt like burning rubber. He didn't like American girls, they way they dressed or acted.

"Oh no I'm quite sure I can find it all by myself."

"I wouldn't dream of allowing a young lady to wander about Paris on her own! Aziz will be discreet."

"But—"

"You'll never know he's there. And it's not just your safety I'm thinking of. You do have a tendency to stir up trouble with your er, imagination."

"He doesn't like me."

"Humph. Doesn't like you. What do you care?"

* * *

"Who's that rather unsavory looking chap following us?" One of the members of The Deadly Dames Book Club asked after introductions had been made on the steps of the Louvre. Including Mrs. Chrisholder, there were seven charter members of the club each dressed in various tweeds and wearing well worn walking shoes. Riley had been introduced as *a young lady Harry's American friend is chaperoning on her first trip to Paris. You know, Harry's American friend, Lou Raferman, the man you all met at Dunphys...*

Mrs. Chrisholder glanced back at Aziz. "No reason for alarm That's Lou's man. A bit of a chauffeur, cook, housekeeper. You name it."

"He's not going to—"

"No. I'm sure he just escorted her over. It is her first time in Paris."

They had all been to the Louvre *countless* times before (hadn't everyone?) so while Riley stumbled through the lobby transfixed in wonder, they marched along purposefully, past groups of newbies studying museum maps, past docents and schoolchildren and straight downstairs with Riley tripping behind them. No dawdling allowed! They were going on a very special tour, Mrs. Chrisholder explained. Not the usual mundane slog through the upper galleries, but downstairs to the antiquities. They were not Agatha Christie fans, as Riley had assumed. Heavens no! The murders in a Christie novel weren't nearly gruesome enough to hold their interest. These rugged, no-nonsense but upper-crust "dames" were in Paris for a self-guided tour of the macabre and grotesque sites of the city, beginning with *horrors from the ancient world* found in the vast labyrinth below the Louvre. They were charter members of the Deadly Dames Society, an order devoted entirely to murder, mayhem, and depravity. In fiction, of course.

At first Riley thought it would be interesting to see the museum through the eyes of Edgar Allen Poe fans; but after the fiftieth piece of clay pottery from the era of Gilgamesh, she couldn't wait for the tour to end. Not so, the Deadly Dames, who moved from exhibit to exhibit like a pack of beagles, noses pressed firmly to the glass, reading every single word, memorizing every titillating detail about ancient torture devices and implements for embalming! Any gruesome artifact that had been used in a death fascinated them endlessly.

"When are we going to see the Mona Lisa?" Riley asked, after they'd finished the basement tour. "After lunch?"

"The Mona Lisa? Everyone comes to the Louvre just to see that small, inconsequential portrait! No, no, my dear. After lunch, we're off to the Catacombs! You don't want to miss that tour! I daresay it's not on the typical tourist route."

She really, really wanted to see the "inconsequential" masterpieces on the upper floor but apparently if she admitted as much Riley would expose herself as a *typical tourist*. And so, she went along with the Deadly Dames figuring that the next day, she could return and see what *she* really wanted to see. The typical tourist crap. The crap she could write home about on cheesy postcards like every other first time visitor to Paris.

To get to the Catacombs, Mrs Chrisholder explained, they would have to take the metro. Oh, they could grab a couple of cabs but where would be the fun in that?

The lower they descended into the bowels of the metro, the more coffin-like it became. The macabre atmosphere only heightened the delight of the seven Deadly Dames. They talked of the murders, kidnappings, rapes and debaucheries that had taken place in the metro with such an unabashed glee, H. P. Lovecraft himself would have been shocked. The deeper they descended, the more aroused they became. Finally they arrived on a crowded platform just as their train pulled in.

"Don't get too settled in," Mrs. Chrisholder warned as they climbed aboard. "We have to change trains at Châtelet-des Halles."

Châtelet-des Halles! The others gasped.

"We can handle it, ladies," Mrs. Chrisholder insisted. "Just keep your bags next to your body. Eyes ever vigilant!"

"What's wrong with Châtelet?" Riley asked.

"Oh," Mrs. Chrisholder began, "it's a very old station, poorly lit, and in desperate need of renovation, thus a haven for pickpockets, rapists, and even worse."

"You've forgotten about the murder."

"Murders!" Mrs. Crisholder corrected. "There was a fresh one just last week! Poor timing for us, dears. We just missed it!"

"What a shame," they all agreed.

After listening to them go on about the horrors of Châtelet, Riley exited the train fully expecting to see Dickensian characters loitering in the shadows, toothless, shabby and reaching out with grubby hands for spare change. But everything looked normal; the only thing frightening was the look on people's faces as they melded into the flow of foot traffic leading to the main station, their bodies programmed by the mind-numbing routine of a daily commute. Something Riley vowed she would never become, a mindless daily commuter.

Once they arrived at the proper platform Mrs. Chrisholder discovered something much to her disgust. The timetable posted on the wall did not match the pamphlet they'd picked up on the way into the station. "How typical! It's no wonder nothing in this bloody country is on time. They can't even coordinate their schedules!"

"Well, what do you expect? If it weren't for our boys, they'd all be wearing swastikas!"

"Which schedule is to be believed? The one on the wall or the one printed in their bloody pamphlets?"

"Who bloody hell knows!"

The rudeness of the Dames soon drew looks of the disgust of the other riders. Riley distanced herself from ladies unfortunately wedging herself between a group of passengers and the incoming train they were desperate to board. As soon as the doors opened, the crowd swelled forward, not even waiting for those on board to depart. She was lifted off her feet and swept forward by the mass.

"Not that train, Miss O'Tannen! It's going the wrong direction," the Dames shouted, but it was too late. She had been pushed, elbowed and kneed onto the wrong train.

CHAPTER 24

THE PICKPOCKET

HE HAD THE DARKEST SKIN she'd ever seen on a human being and stood tall and straight over the other riders "Pickpockets work in groups of three," he said, as they rattled through the dark tunnel. "Two old ones stand in doors to push crowd in, while young, pretty one, like this," he shook the pickpocket until she released the Riley's passport."Grab things and then slip out like rats. Often they look like étudiante, uh, innocent schoolgirls, and then they stick their *leetle* fingers in the pockets, the handbags, where they do not belong! Mon Dieu, they are very good, they are trained from little children."

It had all happened so fast; one minute she'd been struggling to get off the train and the next she'd heard a loud cry: "Pickpocket!" The crowd had frozen. She'd looked down and there stood a little girl in the crisp, clean uniform of a French schoolgirl holding a US passport in her hands. An older woman reached through the crowd to pull the girl from the train but the black man stepped in, grabbing the pickpocket's arm and refusing to let go.. After a violent struggle, the other passengers shoved the older woman from the train. The doors slammed shut and the train blasted off for the next station.

The other passengers, some moaning from injuries sustained during the melee, had moved to the front or rear of the car leaving the dark-skinned man, the petite pickpocket, and the young American alone in the center.

"She's just a child!" Riley said looking into the eyes of the petite dark-haired creature who keep whimpering: *Save me* "Maybe she had no choice. Maybe they were making her steal."

Over the intercom the engineer announced that they were approaching the Saint Jacques station, followed by an automated warning about pickpockets.

"We give her to the police," the black man. said, as the train began slowing. "They are perhaps nicer to her than the other ones. But do not try to save her. She's a gypsy. She cannot change."

"Save me," she pleaded. "Je suis innocent!" Her worm-like fingers clung desperately to Riley's arm. "Innocent!"

"She's just a child!"

The train stopped. Waiting on the platform were three policemen.

"Save me! Please …"

"The police will be nicer to her than the *Roma*," the man repeated as the doors opened. The policemen climbed on board and, without saying a word, grabbed the girl and dragged her backwards out of the train and up the stairs as she wailed like a banshee. Weary commuters barely glanced in her direction as the doors to the other cars opened and people went on their way. Just another day for them.

Riley thanked the man with a shared nod of head and hopped off the train. No more metro for me, she vowed, as she made her way toward the exit. It was a world of commuting zombies, where innocent young girls were forced to pickpocket to live. The rotting core of a beautiful city.

Outside a cold, hard rain fell on the wide boulevard. Although immobilized by complete gridlock and despite the fact that anger would not help, the drivers of vehicles big and small kept leaning on their horns, waving their fists and yelling obscenities. "Imbeciles!" Riley shouted into the rain. "Imbeciles!"

She had no idea where she was but figured she couldn't be too far, maybe three metro stations, from Lou's neighborhood. She could walk it.

"Où est le musée du Louvre?" She asked a friendly-looking man who'd stopped to put up his umbrella.

"Suivez cette route. C'nest pas loin," he replied, pointing down the boulevard.

"Pardon?"

"Perhaps one kilometer. Straight," he replied in almost perfect English. Then he hustled away in the opposite direction.

So many paintings have been done of Paris in the rain, scenes of brightly colored umbrellas unfolding against a grey sky, stylish people walking their stylish dogs, gentlemen sitting at outdoor cafés, smoke from their cigars drifting into a gentle mist. Pure hogwash as far as Riley could tell. Instead of umbrellas, most pedestrians held newspapers over their heads as they ran down the sidewalks rudely shoving others into the oily mess in the gutters. The air smelt of rotting fish and rang of sirens. That was the real Paris in the rain. A noisy mess.

* * *

There was a pot simmering on the stove in the kitchen when she finally arrived at Lou's. Lentil soup, from the looks of it. Spiced with garlic, from the smell. The Moroccan's tiny television set was on, turned to the twenty-four hour horse races he loved to watch, but there was no sign of either man.

"Mr. Raferman," She called out. "Aziz?" No response.

After putting her tennis shoes near the stove to dry, she stole a small cup of soup and had just sat down at the table to watch the horses when she heard the phone ringing in Lou's office, the office she was warned never to enter, the phone she was told never to answer and so she ignored it. Eventually it stopped. Then a few minutes later it started again. Ring, ring, ring. It was so insistent that she began to wonder. Maybe it was her uncle. She ran down the hall and grabbed the receiver.

"Hello? Uncle Bob?"

There was a pause. "Is this Riley?"

"Yes. Who's this?"

"This is Gil," he replied. It was such a shock to hear his voice that she stumbled back into Lou's massive captain's chair.

"Oh."

"You sound funny."

"I'm soaking wet. I'll probably get pneumonia."

"Go get changed; take a rest. It sounds like you need it."

"Shall I tell Lou that you called?"

"No. In fact, never let him catch you in his inner sanctum. He's neurotic about things like that. Hang up now. Hopefully I'll see you soon."

She hung up as ordered and took a look around Lou's precious inner sanctum. On the walnut desk were black-and-white photos of a much younger Lou with various uniformed officers. From their serious expressions she gathered that they were pictures taken during the war. A silver inbox held his file folders; globe style bookends kept a row of leather-bound books upright; colored pens lay ready for use. Nothing out of order except a manila folder lying near the phone. For some reason she flipped it open. Clipped to the inside cover was a picture of a man and woman standing in front of a castle. The woman's face had been whited out. The man had a big square head and sinister face that looked familiar. Aside from the picture, there were several documents all in German. She thought she heard the front door open and so closed the folder and hurried back to kitchen.

But it was nothing. She was still alone in the apartment.

CHAPTER 25

KIDNAPPED

"SHE SLEEPS!"

Riley opened her eyes. Outside it was dark. The rain had stopped.

"She sleeps!" The Moroccan shouted again. Lou appeared a few minutes later in the door. She could only see him in silhouette but she could tell he was livid.

"Where have you guys been?" She asked. After a bit of lentil soup and bread, she'd plopped herself on the daybed and fallen asleep.

"I was investigating your kidnapping!" Lou squealed stomping his foot like an enraged Rumpelstiltskin.

The Deadly Dames had waited for over an hour on the platform at Châtelet des Halles for the young American to return, having made *the logical assumption* that she would return. And when she did not, they called Lou Raferman.

"Miss O'Tannen has been kidnapped!" they reported. "Kidnapped by a giant African who intends to sell her into slavery!"

Unable to calm them down over the phone, Lou dropped what he was doing and drove to Châtelet-des

Halles where the Deadly Dames anxiously awaited his arrival.

"Calm down," he demanded of women much taller than he.

"Calm down?" they asked incredulously. First they'd witnessed the gypsies drag Miss O'Tannen onto a train. And when she did not return (*as expected, as any sensible girl would do, according to Lou*) they assaulted the metro police with their concerns only to learn that there had been a scuffle onboard the train and that a pickpocket had been arrested. Those injured in the scuffle had all reported that a girl matching Miss O'Tannen's description was last seen talking to a large black man. A sex trader from the shores of North Africa, no doubt!

"Think what a sultan would pay for such an addition to his harem as a young blonde girl!" Mrs. Chrisholder cried. "You must contact both the CIA and Interpol! They may be trying to smuggle her out of the country in a boat or perhaps in the back of a truck at this very minute!"

At first Lou tried to talk them down. Perhaps she's just gotten lost in the metro system, he suggested, but Mrs. Chrisholder was insistent, citing incident after incident of young blonde girls disappearing forever, last seen in the company of dark-skinned men. And so reluctantly he'd put his *thirty year* reputation on the line and called in favors.

* * *

"I hear you were kidnapped by a sex slave trader this time," Uncle Bob said. He had called with good news, only to find out that his boss was livid, muttering in a quiet, controlled manner that portended only bad things: *your niece, your bloody niece.*

"I didn't think those ladies would be waiting for me, honest Uncle Bob. I thought they'd keep going on their tour."

"You didn't think they'd be waiting for you? You thought that they'd just say 'la-ti-da' and go ahead with their tour? Well, it *was* nice to have a job."

"Oh, I don't think Lou's that mad. At least he's been very quiet. That is a good sign, isn't it?

"It's a good sign if you want to be stationed in Igloo, South Dakota."

CHAPTER 26

WO IST DIE BIBLIOTEK?

THEY LEFT PARIS THE NEXT DAY in a cold drizzle, escaping, Lou promised, an early snowstorm which would have trapped them in the city forever, something he could not afford as he had an office to run, and besides, his men had done a thorough search of Charlie's car, and found nothing, nothing whatsoever to indicate why the Swiss police would want it returned as evidence in their investigation. Once again he asked Riley if she had something that belonged to Charlie.and once again she replied she could think of nothing. Once again, she was relegated to the backseat while he rode in front with the driver, supposedly so both men could both puff away on their cigarettes without damaging her delicate young lungs. Ha! It was a crock of bull, as her mother would say. Despite multiple apologies, she knew Lou Raferman wanted to strangle her and dump in body is an out of the way alleyway for the rats to dine upon. She'd embarrassed him at his favorite restaurant and almost instigated another international incident. She had to go.

"You're very lucky. Mrs. Chrisholder was amused by your escapade. She said it had added an element of wicked to their trip."

"I'm sure if I actually *had* been abducted and sold to

some sultan it would have made a much better story. If I'd been drugged and raped and found by Interpol chained to a bed on his yacht! Or maybe disfigured, murdered, tortured…"

"Please dear. I have a splitting headache. I can no longer deal with women's imaginations!" With that, he closed the window that separated the driver's compartment from backseat and it was left closed for the rest of the dreary drive.

In Germany it was too cold for snow, if anything fell from the sky it would be ice, or so said the Armed Forces radio network.

"I've got to get right to the office," Lou said as they entered the American section of Worms, "Aziz will drive you out to Gunthersblum. When are you going back to the States?" he asked as he climbed out of the car.

"I missed my return flight and the airline company won't refund my ticket so I don't have enough money — "

"I can get you on a dependent's flight back to the states. I think there's one leaving around Thanksgiving."

"How much will it cost me?"

"I'll pay!!! Aziz, make sure the young lady gets inside the house. I'm still responsible for her until her uncle returns and—"

"I don't plan to go anywhere."

"Just make sure she gets inside the house."

The door to the house in Guthersblum was locked and the VW, missing from the driveway. Uncle Bob never locks the door to his house, Riley thought as she reached through her backpack for the keys. Never. Not even when he went to bed. He must have gotten home from Switzerland and taken the car somewhere but why lock the door? Especially on what had to be the coldest day of the year. Of course, Aziz hadn't waited until she got into the house. He'd stopped just long enough to throw her duffle on the porch and taken off.

She fished around her backpack until realizing the keys were probably buried at the bottom. "Forget this!" She said and dumped the contents onto the concrete porch. Kleenex, lip gloss, books, pens, loose change, toothbrush, deodorant, passport, traveler's checks, candy wrappers all lay scattered on the porch. And, not one but two sets of keys. Well I'll be damned, she thought, I do have some belonging to Charlie Newsome! His keychain!

* * *

The back door of the officers' club swung open and Helmut emerged. He paused a few minutes and then inexplicably walked back into the building. "For crying out loud!" Riley said. Her butt hurt. She'd been perched on the fossilized seat of Charlie's motorbike for what seemed like hours waiting for Helmut to emerge. She didn't want to be seen the Officer's Club during the lunch hour for fear of running into anyone who worked for Lou Raferman but she needed Helmut and so she waited for him to take his break in the alley behind the club.

Helmut reemerged a couple of minutes later. He was about to climb on his motorcycle when one of the waitresses stopped him. They lit cigarettes. They chatted. On and on, while Riley fidgeted. *Come on Helmut, come on! she* thought, *drive away from the damned club.* Finally the waitress glanced at her watch, threw her cigarette to the ground, and reluctantly walked inside the club.

At first Helmut ignored the squeaky *beep, beep, beep* of the dilapidated machine trying to keep up with his masterpiece of German engineering and then he noticed the frowns on the faces of the pedestrians he passed. What sort of person would make such a scene and embarrass him thusly? He turned down an alleyway, spun around and confronted the menace. "Why are you following me?"

The cyclist removed a leather WWII era helmet from her head and shook loose her long blond hair. "It's me … Riley. I need your help."

"Why did you not come into the club instead following me on that piece of shit? "

"It's Charlie's Newsome bike. He left it at my uncle's. Did you hear about his death?"

"Naturlich."

"Well, I think he might have been killed."

Helmut's eyes narrowed. "I do not have time for this!" he scowled, "I must go to class. Tell your story to polizei. And stop following me!"

"But I have something I think Lou Raferman is looking for."

"I don't understand."

"Your university has a library, right?"

"Naturlich!"

"I need to use one of those microfiche machines."

"Why?"

"To look at some tiny bits of film."

"Film?"

"Yes. I found them in the cylinder attached to his key-chain. It's a long story."

That piqued his interest. "Okay. I will take you to library. Then I have class. I cannot be bothered."

"Great! Wo ist die Bibliotek? Now there's a phrase I never thought I'd ever have to use! Won't Herr Assmus be happy?"

He looked at her as if he already doubted his decision to get involved and then motioned her to follow him.

They crossed over the Roman bridge and took the backroads down to Mannheim where Helmut's university sat as regally as the Baroque palace it had once been. After the first world war, Helmut explained, it had be converted to a business school but only for the best pupils, the very best and most worthy. Like him.

At the door to the vast library he hesitated.

"Danke." Riley said.

"I will stay to see the film."

Yeah, right, she thought. *I bet you're hoping it contains something nice and juicy you can use against us corrupt, imperialist Americans. Some evidence that Lou Raferman, Charlie Newsome and even Uncle Bob are CIA agents.* "How about your class?"

"The first part is review. I can miss."

In a way she was relieved. She'd never used a microfiche machine so having him around was worth putting up with his ego. He turned on his charm with the librarian who made sure they had one of the newer machines and that he knew how to use it. Watching him, Riley knew, without a doubt, Helmut was going to be a captain of industry one day, with multiple homes, a vineyard in France, a Lamborghini, and probably a few yachts. She was certain that one day she'd read an article about him in the Wall Street Journal and think to herself, some tortured poet he turned out to be!

* * *

The first piece of film contained two images: a pencil drawing of a woman in a striped uniform sitting on a wooden chair staring into the distance with a blank expression on her face. There was a similar drawing of a man. They looked healthy and clean but the artist was careful not to portray any emotion, too careful. It was as if they were robots.

"Jews." Helmut explained. "See the stars." He was referring to the roughly cut six-cornered star sewn onto their uniforms. "The Star of David."

"The artist was in a concentration camp?"

Helmut didn't respond. He flipped quietly to the other piece of film which contained images of spread sheets.

"This is not possible!" he barked. "It cannot be."

"What do you mean?"

"These are Swiss. Swiss bank statements."

"How do you know?"

"I'm a business student. My interest is in all things commercial."

"Who do they belong to?"

"This is impossible to know. They only have customer number, no name," He pulled a small notebook from his satchel and began writing down numbers from the screen. "Herr Newsome had a lot of money."

"I can't believe they belonged to Charlie. He worked for the army. They must belong to someone else."

"I do not know." Helmut said as he continued writing down numbers. Then he abruptly stood up and informed her that she had wasted enough of his valuable time.

CHAPTER 27

THE SLOPPY AMERICAN

"IT'S MY NIECE'S FAULT that we're late, Roger. She's discovered a *spy* in our midst."

"I didn't know you'd invited us to dinner. Honest, Mr. Saski. When I got home from Paris, Uncle Bob was gone and so I —"

"And so you decided to hop on Charlie's old bike and figure out what got him killed!"

Simone and her husband lived in a cluster of older homes down on the river. Roger'd greeted them at the front door and then led them to a living room at the back of the house. "I thought Newsome died of a heart attack." He said as he invited them to take a seat.

"He did. But my niece discovered old Charlie's se-cret..." Uncle Bob stopped and looked around the room. "Where's Simon? She's gotta hear this story!"

"Finishing dinner. I hope you like lamb and couscous. Ever since we got back from Tangiers, *Simone* uses any excuse she can to make lamb."

"Is that where you got all these masks? Tangiers?" Riley asked, referring to the tribal masks on the walls.

"Yes, anything African she just loves. Don't even get her started on Ray Charles."

"I should go help her in the kitchen."

"Oh, no. French women do not allow *anyone* in their kitchens when they are preparing dinner. Especially, the guests! Stay seated, and I'll get the champagne and escargot."

As soon as Roger was out of the room, Uncle Bob said: "Death masks on the walls.? Humm. Maybe the Saskis are spies too. Or maybe they're cannibals!"

"Knock it off!"

Their host returned seconds later with gold-rimmed flutes of chilled champagne and a tray of hors d'oeuvres. In addition to the snails, there was an assortment of olives and stuffed mushrooms.

"I had Simon make these snails especially for you."

"Uncle Bob—You did not!"

"No, I didn't," he admitted, "but just smother them in the melted butter and that's all you'll taste, the butter. You trust your old unc, don't you, Niecey?"

"She doesn't like escargot?"

"Of course I do, Roger. Look, I'm going to eat one." She washed down the snail with a half glass of champagne.

"You're not really supposed to swallow it whole but it's okay my dear; they aren't for everyone. Now what's all this about Newsome?" Roger lowered himself into a high backed chair across from them and light a cigarette. "He could really make a nuisance of himself and that's a fact. There are certain ways to behave in, um certain situations which, despite all his years in Europe, he never quite figured out."

"Yeah, the poor sod probably thought he was in love with your wife."

"Exactly. He was so damn sloppy."

"That's what we American boys are, Rog, sloppy."

Riley had heard about the sloppy American from Jean-Jacques, the happy hour expert on American sexual hang-ups. It was his favorite topic of conversation. The sloppy American can't separate love from lust and thus ends up creating unnecessary *messiness*. Like most American girls, Riley was hobbled by the mores of her puritan ancestors, lulled into believing in fairy-tale love by Disney fairy tales and thus prevented from enjoying uncomplicated sex. In Europe, married people were expected to take lovers, without the great stigma that the puritanical Americans applied to extramarital sex. Getting a new lover was almost like getting a dog or cat, or maybe a new purse. No big deal. This made Frenchmen more romantic, and, naturellement, better lovers.

"Well, not all American boys." Roger rose to fill the Riley's empty glass. "So what makes you think Charlie was a spy? By the way, champagne should be sipped and not guzzled."

"Wait. First tell Roger how Lou had half of Interpol looking for you while you were sleeping in his den."

"Oh, Uncle Bob, that's such an exaggeration. It was just a misunderstanding."

"Ok, I'm lost."

"Let's wait until dinner. I don't want Simon to miss the fun."

"By all means, Bob."

Simone Saski's dining room table was a work of art . She'd paired cut crystal wine goblets in all colors of the rainbow with bone white china upon which a cassoulet of steaming French onion soup awaited each of them. Silver candle holders in every corner of the small room, reflected light in the mirrored wallpaper.

"Wow. You've really outdone yourself!" Riley said, taking a seat across from her uncle while their hosts sat at either end of the table.

"Outdone myself?"

"She means this isn't how we do dinner at the Neilson house."

"Ha. I'll say! I'm sorry I look such a fright. I was ..."

"It is not a problem. And Paris? How was Paris?"

"Well, it sure is a big city and crowded. But the downtown is nice."

"Nice? Did you go to the Louvre? It's very close to Monsieur Raferman's place, non?"

"Simone's been dying to see Lou's place. She's green with envy."

"Roger!"

"Well it's not that fancy but it is close to a lot of things. And I did get to the Louvre but I went with his friend and she was only interested in the stuff in the basement. I didn't even get to see the Mona Lisa!"

"For Pete's sake! We don't want to hear about the damned Mona Lisa. Tell the Saskis about the kidnapping!"

The story of Riley's "kidnapping" entertained the Saskis through the most of the meal.

"Now, young lady. How did you come to the conclusion that Charlie was a spy?" Roger asked as his wife laid out an assortment of cheeses and fruit.

"Well, Lou kept asking me if Charlie'd given me anything. And I kept telling him "no," but I forgot I still had the keys to the Fiat."

"The keys to his car?"

"Yes, I drove through Switzerland so I had the keys and Lou never asked me about them; he just had Charlie's car towed. And then I remembered that Helmut, you know the bartender at the Club? Well he goes to Mannheim University and universities have libraries and libraries have those machines that can read tiny bits of film."

"Microfiche? And why did you need a microfiche machine?"

"Oh the film in the cylinder on the keychain. Helmut didn't want to help me at first but then he got curious."

"Naturally. Like most Germans, the bartender thinks we DACs are all involved in all manner of clandestine activities. We're all *the third man*. And what was on this film?"

After Riley told them what she'd seen, Simone exchanged glances with her husband. "I think we can answer part of this mystery."

"Yes, sadly. I think you are right, mon cherie."

"Really? Would this have to do with his first wife? The one he saved from the concentration camps?"

"Yes, that's right, Riley," Roger said. "Her father was an artist —"

"With the Montparnasse!" Simone added.

"Yes dear. Charlie claimed his father-in-law was forced

to create portraits of the prisoners that made them look healthy and well-fed, which the prison commandants would give to the Red Cross. You know, as proof that the concentration camps weren't so bad. It's a sick business, war. But many of those drawings disappeared after the liberation. Ariel — that was his first wife — wanted to forget everything about the camps but Charlie became obsessed, especially when he heard that someone was selling them on the black market. He probably heard it from Raferman."

"Highly unlikely. You know how Lou feels about dealing with Nazi hunters. I'm sure he wants to get his hands on whatever Charlie had so that he can put the matter to bed."

"You're right Bob."

"What happened to Ariel?"

"She wanted to move to the States but Charlie wasn't having any of it. Probably because he'd starting carrying on with that Parisian model."

Simone began clearing the table. "And now, it is over. No more talk of the war and the camps."

Poor Helmut, Riley thought. How disappointed he will be when I tell him that Charlie's mission was a personal one, not at all involved with spying or the CIA. He was just a sad man trying to expose the people who did an injustice to a woman he himself had cheated on. What a sloppy mess indeed.

After dinner they had coffee, cognac, and petit fours in the living room. A full moon had come out from behind the thin cloud layer and now reflected in the river below.

In order to fully enjoy the scene, Uncle Bob and Simone decided to take a stroll down to the river bank with their cognacs. Riley begged off because she still felt a cold coming on and Roger begged off because of an old war injury.

"So poor Charlie was just trying to make amends to his first wife. How romantic," Riley said, "and how sad."

"Well, in a way. Not to be too cynical but there was the financial angle. Messerman's work is now worth a fortune. Much more than his daughter is going to get from the army, if they ever find her."

"How old would she be?"

"I imagine about your age. Still a kid. You know, we were just kids back then. Kids, far from home. We made a lot of mistakes, some of which are hard to make amends for."

"When did you meet Charlie?"

"Oh, about ten…fifteen years ago, here in Worms. His wife was a Parisian and she was not happy about being based in Germany, not happy at all. Of course, none of us were, but you know, it's where the job was. Simone tried to be friends with her but it was impossible. Parisians have a tendency to look down their noses at a *provinciale*. Besides, Simone was a good deal younger. She was a child during the war, you know."

He took another swig of cognac.

"How did you get over to Europe?" Riley asked. The cognac stung going down but cleared her clogged sinuses so nicely that she helped herself to a second glass.

"Oh…I was shoved. Shoved out of a plane in the

middle of the night along with a bunch of other clod-hoppers. I remember some scarecrow…a real hick from the sticks, sitting across from me reminiscing about his ma's cherry pies. Cherry pies she's cooking, in some cozy kitchen while her baby boy is about to be shoved out into the cold sky."

He took another long drag on his cigarette. "You think things like that when you're about to die—you know, you wonder if you'll be missed by somebody. My finger-tips were black, I'd smoked every Camel I had right down to the end and singed my skin. Everyone had. The smell in that plane was something I'll never forget; a sick-ly combination of cigarette smoke, burning oil, and of all things, aftershave lotion! I remember just sitting there and thinking what kind of a schmuck doses himself in after-shave before being dropped out a plane? Did they think sexy French women would be waiting for them when they hit the ground? Ha!"

Riley watched as the ring of smoke encircled his head like the years gone by. Not that he was an old man, not really, probably thirty five. She wondered if she should say something but what?

"Unfortunately for those wannabe Romeos, there was a big fire in the town that night that lit up the night sky, making us easy pickings for the Krauts."

He stood and walked over to the window where he stood quietly taking in the moonlight. "Thank God, I was a skinny little fart else I wouldn't be here today."

CHAPTER 28

THE BURGERMEISTER

"TELEPHONE!" THE PUTZIE SCOWLED.

One eye was caked shut with mucus and the other, glued to the pillowcase. Riley knew that if she tried to lift her head, it would fall off. "Tell whoever it is to call back."

"Jetzt!" She ordered. "Need air! You stink!" She said stomping over to the window.

"Don't open the window1 It's freezing outside!"

"You stink!"

"Go away!"

"Ist Oncle Boob!" The Putzie snapped. "Ach! Du bist eine Wino"

"Who do you think you are? Meine Mutti? Go away!"

"Nein. Telephone. Oncle Boob. Jetzt."

"Okay, just go away! I'll come."

"Jetzt!"

"Alright, I'm coming. Go away."

Riley stood up slowly putting one hand on the bed frame for support. The room spun around her. She sat back down again.

* * *

"Niecey," Uncle Bob ordered after she managed to propel herself downstairs to the phone, "Pour yourself a glass of tomato juice, add a couple of teaspoons Tabasco sauce, some black pepper, and if you can handle it, a raw egg. And then drink it—fast."

"What are you talking about? I hate tomato juice!"

"You're hungover. Tomato juice is the best remedy for what ails you."

"I don't have a hangover. I'm sick."

"You don't say? Good, then meet me at Lou's office."

"Why?"

"Maybe he misses you. Anyway, it's not a request. It's an order."

"I don't work for him!"

"Yes, but I do and you owe me. Besides he wants Charlie's keychain and that film. I forgot to get it from you this morning."

"Oh and he can't wait until I at least take a shower."

"No. You have to get that keychain down here PDQ."

Snow had fallen overnight, nonetheless, all of the windows in the house were open and the bedding flung over the ledges. As long as the sun was out, the bedding got aired.

Riley dressed as quickly as she could under the circumstances, swallowed a couple of aspirins, grabbed a piece of Wonder Bread and her backpack.

"You're insane!" She shouted at the Putzie. "Absolutely, positively insane! It's freezing outside!"

155

Snow hadn't slowed the Putzie's maniacal quest for freshly aired bedding but it had slowed traffic to a crawl. The twenty minute drive into town took nearly an hour and a half. By the time she reached Lou's office, the two aspirins she'd taken were already wearing off.

"Sit," Lou ordered, after closing the door. His Worms office had no personality whatsoever, just Army-issued furniture and a view, not of the Seine, but of the dreary landscape of the base. Lou was also dressed more conservatively than before, no ascot or monogrammed handkerchief, no pearl cufflinks, no flashy scarf. Just a plain old everyday dark-blue suit, starched white shirt and striped tie.

He looked up at her from behind an immaculate desk. "You look...terrible. What's wrong with your eyes? "

"I have a cold. I may even have pink eye," She replied pulling a wet Kleenex from the pocket of her jeans and taking a seat across from him.

"For God's sakes, don't touch anything! I'll be brief. The reason I needed to speak to you, Miss O'Tannen, is that the burgermeister of Worms—a royal asshole!—had only one child. A daughter. Unfortunately, killed in a motorcycle accident early this morning."

"What's a burgermeister exactly. A mayor?"

"Not all burgermeisters are elected, like a mayor. Some inherit the title, which makes them think they're better than a lowly elected official. In some occasions, they're not just the mayor of the biggest town in their region but of all the towns nearby, giving them the rank of a *provincial magistrate*."

Lou turned to Uncle Bob who stood uncharacteristically quiet in the corner. "Why am I telling your niece all this? I didn't ask her down here to give her a lesson in German civics, did I?"

He merely shrugged his shoulders.

"She's on a mission to destroy me, isn't she?"

"Really Mr. Raferman. You're being just a tad hysterical."

"A tad hysterical? The reason I asked you down here, young lady, is that the burgermeister's daughter was killed while riding on the back of a motorcycle driven by her beau, who just happened to be the bartender at *our* officers' club! He is, unfortunately, also deceased."

"Oh my God, Helmut."

"Yes, Helmut, that sounds right. Helmut."

"That's awful but—"

"What does this have to do with you, you might ask?"

"Yeah."

"Didn't I ask you if Charles Newsome had given you something before he died?"

"Yes, but I didn't realize you were talking about the key chain. It's such a little thing."

"Did I say I was looking for a big thing?"

"Well, no."

He paused a second to collect himself. "Okay, my dear, just give me the key chain and we'll be done with this whole sordid business."

"So you knew all about Charlie…"

"Yes, of course, I bloody well knew. It was an obsession of his! Luckily for him, he died believing he had the evidence to finally get justice. Justice! Lord God, what a sloppy affair justice is."

"I don't understand what this has to do with the burgermeister."

"Apparently before his accident, Helmut told the burgermeister about the film, and so now the idiot thinks his daughter was killed by the CIA!"

"Oh. Well, can't you just tell him about Charlie's obsession?"

"Since Newsome's obsession was with him, I hardly think that the correct course. The key chain, please. I do have a full schedule."

"I don't understand. It was the Burgermeister—"

"We have fairly good, though not conclusive, evidence that the esteemed burgermeister of Worms began his career as a guard at a concentration camp. How Newsome got wind of it I don't know, but once he found out, well, there was no stopping him and he was hardly the soul of discretion. The key chain, please."

"What a strange coincidence that his daughter's boyfriend worked at the—"

"The key chain, please. I'm most anxious to put this sordid affair behind me."

"Sure, it's in my backpack." She picked up the backpack from the floor and dumped the contents on his desk.

"Good Lord! Haven't you ever heard of a trash can?" His pristine desk was now piled high with used Kleenex, hair-filled brushes, a dirty toothbrush, loose aspirin, chap stick, rubber bands and receipts.

"The backpack *is* her trash can!"

Once, twice, three times, Riley searched through the debris while Lou fidgeted. "Well, it was here yesterday. I must have taken it out last night and put it someplace safe."

"Someplace safe?" Lou glared at Uncle Bob.

"Don't look at me! She drove home from the Saski's last night and she was in fine shape, let me tell you! I went out this morning and the VW was parked smack dab in the middle of the road!"

CHAPTER 29

PASSING THE HAT

DEATH SOURED THE MOOD at happy hour that night as the regulars spoke of Helmut, the oft invisible young man who studied them cynically while perfecting their martinis, for he was an ambitious and flexible German, willing to cater to their desires in order to further his dreams. An acceptable German. A capitalistic German, now gone too young, in a ridiculous accident, probably driving too fast (don't all young people?) on such a dangerous machine, over icy roads, late at night. Not much was known about the girl with him except that she was the daughter of the local potentate—what was his name? Oh yes—Dradon, Kert Dradon. Wasn't he some sort of Nazi during the war? Weren't they all? Yes, but this one. Well now, he's the grand pooh-bah. Ha. The burgermeister, that's what they're called. We should have hung them all when we had the chance.

The hat, a plastic plate on which folded fives were dominant, went round for a younger brother of Helmut's, no mention of the parents. Then they went on to that other untimely death.

"Dang, but he could be a pain," the general began. "Still, only fifty-five, much too young to die. Did anyone really know him that well? No? Well, he was a vet, served his country admirably; that's all anyone really needs to know."

There'd be no hat for Charlie, as there was no family left behind in need; only a daughter who seemed to have disappeared.

The bartender struggling to take Helmut's place acted as though the regulars would eat him alive if he got their orders wrong. He lacked the arrogance of Helmut, the barely beneath-the-surface contempt for his customers. But all seated at the bar agreed, this new lad would learn, yes indeed. And if he could make a good martini—he would be kept. Don't worry, young lad, heh, heh. It's easier than you think.

Riley had been waiting for her uncle for over an hour wondering what people would say if they knew there *might* be a connection between the two deaths. But Lou had made it painfully clear that she must not read anything into what she'd heard in his office. It was all a minor misunderstanding between two men which was now over. A consequence of the war that must be put in the past. She would be extremely remiss if she "shot off her mouth" at the Officers' Club!

Finally her uncle arrived, "Fritzy, that's your name is it?" He asked the bartender. "Bring me a Heineken with a whiskey chaser, bitte schön."

"Uncle Bob, I've got some bad news. I can't find that keychain. I looked all over the house and the car and —"

"Have you seen Simone?" He asked.

"No…"

He turned his back on her and greeted the blonde who'd

slid in next to him at the bar. "Hi Bobby," she purred in a low and sexy voice as she climbed up onto the barstool and crossed her long tan legs.

"You're a sight for sore eyes," he said.

"You must be Bob's niece," she said reaching over to shake Riley's hand, "I'm Annie."

"Yes. I remember you from my first night here."

"Right! Gads, this whole Newsome affair makes me feel so old," she sighed, tapping her cigarette on the bar.

"You look great! How do you stay so thin with all these peanuts and French fries?"

"I look a lot sexier five pounds thinner, don't I?" she asked the gruff looking man who stood possessively behind her. "This is my husband."

"Yes, you do," he concurred.

"Hell, I'd look a lot sexier *fifty* pounds lighter," Uncle Bob laughed. "So would you, Dougie."

Dougie growled and turned to the bartender.

What a creep, Riley thought. *It's a good thing Uncle Bob said something before I did.*

"Let me tell you about my day, Annie. It's been a real triumph. Oh yeah. Wouldn't you agree, Niecey? We were going over the quarterlies when the burgermeister came marching into Lou's office. You know the fella, Annie. His face is as unlined as a baby's butt!"

Annie's fingers quivered as she lit a cigarette and exhaled slowly. "Who is he?"

"Come on, you've seen the guy. He comes to the club every now and then to give us a speech about German-American relations—how we should all get along, blah,

blah, blah. Don't tell me you've missed his speeches? I'll have to have my niece here give you a lecture about proper American behavior in an occupied country."

She giggled. "Oh, that guy. He's had work done in Switzerland. He gets injections of goat embryonic fluid —they're all the rage, don't you know?"

"You don't say?"

"That's what I heard. What did he want with Lou?"

"Well, for one thing, he didn't want Lou. He wanted my niece!"

"Your niece?"

"Yeah, he thinks she's some kind of CIA agent!"

"Why?"

"Oh, it's too ridiculous to even talk about. I'm sure you'll read about it in the papers which is where he threatened to spread his bullshit."

"Oh boy! Can't wait!"

Dougie turned and abruptly announced: "Woman, I'm hungry. Gather your brood and cook me up some pork chops. I'll be home in a half hour."

Mumbling a "pardon me," she climbed off her perch, and did as ordered.

"You have nothing to be pardoned for!" Riley said as her uncle cautioned her to say no more.

* * *

Uncle Bob was quiet after Annie left, downing bottle after bottle of Heineken as Riley nursed a tall glass of orange juice. She'd vowed, after waking up in such pain to never, never drink alcohol again.

Finally he spoke: "Something's come up, Niecey. I

have to go to Paris tomorrow morning to try to talk some sense into your aunt."

"What?"

"Your aunt, she's moved to Paris. Look what came in the mail today." He handed her a letter on rose-colored stationery. The handwriting rounded and soft with little heart's dotting the i's.

She did a quick scan of the contents and returned it to him."I can't read this, Uncle Bob—it's so personal."

"Oh hell. Let's let the whole world hear what she has to say, and *sooooo eloquently*! Listen to this everyone:

Stephano doesn't see me as fat and disgusting—but adores, passionately, my whole body. He knows how to please a woman and for such a young man, is wise beyond his years. And let me tell you, he could have any woman! Any woman! He's so gorgeous and muscular. But it's me he wants. Hopefully we can get our divorce over rapidly so I can marry him. He just can't wait!"

Riley sat in horror as her uncle read what should have been a very private, personal letter to the general who hated hippies; to Elke, the German girl in search of an American husband; to Jean Luc, the pasty Frenchman in search of a lay; and to Fritz, the frightened bartender.

"Sounds like she's shakin' the sheets with a goddamn deserter, Bob," the general snarled. "Like the slimy piece of trash my daughter Tami attracted a few years ago. Wanted to marry Tami real quick, move to America. Don't worry; I'll take care of him, Bob, I'll take care of this Stephano just like I took care of Luigi."

"No thanks. I'll take care of it."

"Why don't I come with you to Paris, Uncle Bob? I'm a woman. I can talk to her woman to woman."

"Thanks, but this is my mess to clean up. Besides, I talked to Simone this morning—they've invited you to go with them to Normandy for a few days. It's the Armistice —Roger's annual chance to hang out with his old war buddies. You can keep her company."

"But Lou wants to send me right home. He said he was going to put me on the first plane…"

"Oh yeah. I forgot to tell you. Roger found Charlie's key chain. It must have dropped out of your backpack at their house. Lou has it now."

"What's he going to do with it?"

"Don't ask. I didn't. As far as he's concerned, the matter is closed."

"How can the matter be closed if two people have died? If this Burgermeister guy—"

"Riley, just forget it. Trying to right all the wrongs of the past war is a fool's errand."

That evening she hid in her room writing letters home as downstairs her uncle pleaded with his wife over the phone. It was true, he was a crude and unfaithful husband. It was true that he drank too much and had probably said and done things he shouldn't Maybe he'd even commented on all the weight she'd put on while they'd been in Europe. But she'd never gone to college or even held a job. What if life with Stephano didn't work out?

She tried not to listen but the anger and pain seemed to go on for hours until finally it was quiet.

In the still dark of morning once again she heard the

165

familiar "Sloop, sloop, sloop" of McKuen's ending ode to lost love and went downstairs to cover her uncle with a blanket.

The fat yellow cat had vanished.

CHAPTER 30

ARMISTICE

AT FIRST THE HORSE cantered along the beach pulling the one-man cart behind him as if it was nothing, the bundled figure sitting on the cart rarely raising the whip. Back and forth in front of the hotel they trotted, each time moving closer to the water until finally the horse was knee deep in the lapping waves. By now he had stopped cantering and labored just to pull the cart through the water as the driver raised the whip again and again.

"Poor horse," Riley said. "Why is the man being so cruel?"

Simone looked up from her newspaper. "He is not being cruel. He is training. Is good for legs to train in water. Makes them stronger."

"Well, I'm sure the horse doesn't feel that way!"

With a heavy sigh, the older woman pointed out that Normandy was country.. They didn't have the luxury of caring what the animals thought.

"Oh."

They were staying at a small fishing village which Simone'd chosen over nearby Bayeux or Caen because she liked the quiet pace of fishing villages. She liked to watch the colorful boats chugging out to sea as the sun came up and then returning in the afternoon to moor in the cluttered harbor next to the hotel. She liked the way families in the village spontaneously appeared on the beach whenever the sun shone, playing informal games of soccer with whatever they could find to kick around. They were true and stout Normans.

They'd dropped Roger off early that morning at Omaha Beach to join other WWII vets. First, he planned to volunteer at the various WWII museums in the area, primarily to answer questions or tell stories to visitors. Something he'd been doing on a yearly basis since the end of the war. Then there would be a solemn ceremony at the American cemetery.

"Doesn't it ever get boring for him? To do the same thing year after year?" Riley had asked Simone.

"Oh no. He likes to tell people how he jumped from the plane. Many men died, so, so many. Many more, never the same again. They cannot forget, things so terrible they cannot share with wives. Is good they have each other, no?"

"I guess."

Their hotel was popular with the locals but not in any guidebook or on any tourist route, which, the Riley suspected, was by design. She got the feeling that the owners did just fine catering all the local weddings, anniversaries, and civic events and didn't really worry about keeping the five or six spacious suites above the restaurant occupied. They saved them for outsiders who'd heard of the place via word-of-mouth or banquet guests who'd over-imbibed. To the north guests could see Pointe du Hoc, a sheer cliff rising from the sea. And to the south—if the fog wasn't too bad—the mist-shrouded Cotentin Peninsula. But it was the mural dominating the southern wall of the restaurant that drew most people's attention. A floor-to-ceiling depiction of the siege of Pointe du Hoc, D-Day, June 6, 1944. Men scaling a vertical cliff as bullets and bombs rained down on them. Bodies falling from ropes, flying off the canvas towards the viewer, so lifelike that one expected to find blood splatterings on the white-clothed tables.

"Is this where you met Roger?" She asked after they'd discussed their plans for the rest of the day. If the weather stayed clear, they'd drive down the coast to the town of Cherbourgh and return the inland route through Mere St. Anglaise.

"No, I was a small child when the GIs landed in Normandy. Too young to remember anything other than the lack of food, especially sugar. We lived in the Alsace, close to Germany, not far from Le Petit Dauphin."

"So you didn't see any of the fighting?"

She picked at her lunch. Quietly separating the chicken from the Pommes frites and then just nibbling a bit of the meat and none of the fries. The sudden death of Charles de Gaulle had cast a shadow over her, as well as the whole of France.

"Mon Dieu, many died in the Alsace but I was very young. I remember hiding in the basement. Then when it is finally quiet, some children, they, how do you say it? They followed the blood in the creeks to the battleground and returned with watches, shoes—anything to sell. They steal from the bodies, but not me. No. Not me. I would rather starve!" She took another long drag on her pencil-thin cigarette, gently blowing smoke towards the pane glass windows. "I met Roger after the war. He finds me when I am just a skinny, skinny kid, very hungry. Yes, very hungry. He took care of my family. Then, when I am old enough, we get married."

She imagined Simone with long red braids, her nose covered in freckles, her small feet shoeless, tears rolling down her cheeks as her stomach growled. Too proud to rob the bodies of the dead.

"Is that why you married him, because he saved your family?"

It was, again, the wrong thing to say.

"No, I love him. Maybe not the way you Americans think of love. All fireworks. Marriages are about, how do you say? Trust? This fireworks love is like chocolat. You do not want to eat it every day."

"Of course I do. Chocolate every day. Why not?"

"Chérie, too much chocolat and you will get fat."

"I don't think I could ever settle for just trust."

"I did not say it was just trust." she turned to scan the horizon. They'd heard from the waitress that a storm was moving in from the English Channel. According to Simone, such storms were unpredictable and often violent, washing away roads and bringing down trees. They'd already scuttled their original plan to visit Mont Saint-Michel. "Perhaps we also cancel trip to Cherbourg."

"But it doesn't look that bad." How could the long band of fluffy white clouds hanging above the horizon disguise something malignant? The families picnicking on the beach, the soccer players jostling with each other over the ball, the small children running barefoot into the waves, even the seagulls suspended by cross breezes as they searched for scraps—none of them seemed concerned. None of them—

"Look, chérie. The boats…" A line of fishing boats chugged towards the shore like ducklings following their mother. They didn't seem to be in any particular hurry.

"Maybe the fishing's not good."

As the boats drew nearer, people on the shore began to take note. *Why were the boats coming in so early? It was just past noon.* Eyes turned to the end of the breakwater where the beacon had abruptly come to life, sending flashes of bright orange light in all directions. Startled by the light, the horse pulling the cart reared, dumping its trainer into the waves. He grabbed the harness and began pulling the agitated animal back towards the beach. Parents began shouting to their children, gathering belongings and heading toward the seawall. At first there was no panic but then the church bells began ringing, not in the orderly way that denoted each passing hour, but like a heartbeat run amok.

The proprietress of the hotel rushed to the window, and then quickly turned to members of her staff: *Allez, allez!!*

They responded by running outside to pull the shutters over the windows and retrieve lounge chairs from the veranda.

Simone rose from the table, "I have to get to Roger."

"Shouldn't we wait until the storm blows over?"

"I must be with Roger."

"But our room's on the second floor. Certainly the water won't—"

"No, it is Roger. I told him we go to Saint-Michel. He will not know we change our plans. His heart, Riley, it is not strong."

"Can't we call him?"

She looked at her watch: "They are at American Cemetery now. Impossible to call."

"Okay. Okay. But I'm not staying here alone. I'll go with you."

"Bien."

The proprietress, a Madame D'Isgny, stopped them at the bottom of the staircase. From what Riley could understand, she was begging Simone to return to her room to ride out the storm.

"No!"

"Mais, Madame—"

"No!"

While they argued Riley ran upstairs to grab her jacket. The door to their suite was wide open, which was not how they'd left it that morning. Someone was foraging through the room, grumbling under his breath in German as he did.

CHAPTER 31

NUMERAL DU INCIDENT

THE LOCAL GARDIEN DE LA PAIX—pimply, tall and wearing a uniform that looked like it had been passed down to him by a much fatter conscript—removed his wet slicker, draped it over an empty chair, and sat down across from Riley. He was young, probably her age, but determined to act much older.

"Mademoiselle. Please be brief with your story," he said curtly. The storm (which had raged for five full hours) had kept him hopping from one road closure to the next, rescuing *les idiots* who'd gone out in the maelstrom despite the warnings and, even though the storm was finally moving inland, his ordeal was not over. No, he could not return home until he'd responded to every call for help. The phone lines had been the first to go down but there were still plenty of *Le Resistance* members, stubbornly relying on shortwave radios for communication. The owners of the hotel were among that proud group.

He grasped the cup of tea he'd been given with both hands for warmth, as the ambulance transporting Simone to a hospital in Bayeaux wailed in the distance. *Whoop, whoop, whoop, whoop*—an eerie sound in the post-storm quiet. They'd had to wait for hours for the ambulance to

173

arrive. sitting in the freezing lobby of the hotel as Simone drifted in and out of consciousness.

"Well," Riley began. "The burgermeister chased us here from Worms. I think his name is Kert Dradon or something like that. It's all kind of complicated and I don't understand the whole thing myself, but I saw him in our room and then he must have followed us because suddenly he was trying to push Madame Saski's car off the cliff. That's how she got hurt. And probably he would have done it too, if I hadn't shot at his car. I didn't want to kill him. I don't believe in guns!"

The gardien sighed. He was lost. Riley repeated the whole story, slowly this time. He still looked confused and so she found Madame D'Isgny in the kitchen gathering lanterns and begged her to translate. The electricity would be out for a long time and their generator must be spared for only critical tasks. Please Madam, Riley urged. Bien. Une moment only!

After Madame D'Isgny finished translating, the gardien turned to Riley: "You and Madame Saski went out in the storm because these Nazi was in your room?"

"No, we went to find Monsieur Saski. The burgermeister must have followed us." She wanted to tell him how the car had slid off the road in the heavy rain and stalled and how Simone had flooded the engine trying to restart it. She wanted to tell him how the Burgermeister caught up with them and, while they were *completely* helpless, tried to ram the car off the cliff. But the gardien clapped his notebook shut: "I go now. So many accidents. Are you sure the Nazi did not perhaps, *slid* into your car?

The road, it was...um...slick."

"No. He was definitely trying to push us off the cliff. He was trying to kill us."

"Where did you get the pistol, mademoiselle?"

"It dropped out of the glove compartment after he hit the car the first time. It must belong to Monsieur Saski."

"An American."

"Oui. A veteran."

The gardien rose stiffly and grabbed his slicker. "Je suis fini, mademoiselle."

"But he tried to kill us. You have to arrest him!"

He lifted one eyebrow, "I am a gardien de la paix, mademoiselle. I do not arrest because there is an accident in a bad storm."

"An accident? No. He hit us on purpose. Madame Saski is in the hospital because of him..."

"As is the German," he said, thumbing through his notebook. "Oui. Kert Dradon of Worms. I put zees man in ambulance myself."

"You mean I shot him? I just meant to scare him away really."

"No, he was not shot. His car left the road *à ou près de* three thirty and went into the side of a house. He will live. *Mais*, I can assure you, he will stay in the hospital many days." He shook his slicker and rolled it into a ball. The rain had stopped. "And tonight I am tired. Too many accidents today."

She followed him out to his mud-spattered scooter to try once again. "But the burgermeister tried to kill us!"

"Mademoiselle, contact the regional police if you

want to file a complaint. Perhaps you want to sue. That is what all Americans want to do—sue! But I cannot help with these." He wrote a number on a piece of paper and handed it to her. "Votre numeral du incident."

Riley watched as the gardien de la paix slid down the road on his scooter. She was hoping to witness the nincompoop lose control and fall into the mud. But he didn't. He just puttered off to his next "incident" report. What a useless man he was, she thought, I should have gone in the ambulance with Simone instead of staying behind to meet with him. What am I going to do now? The phones are out, as is the electricity. Possibly, they said, for three days. The only way to reach people was via Madame D'Isgny's shortwave radio which was currently being used only for *emergency* calls.

* * *

That night Riley ate fish chowder in the kitchen along with the rest of the hotel guests. They ate in the kitchen instead of the dining room to stay warm, gathering around a battered wooden table that had probably been used to yank fish guts and peel scales. But it was food and, thanks to a massive wood burning stove, it was hot. The hotel's old generator, despite coaxing and prayers, was only able to sputter along for short periods of time, not nearly long enough to warm the upstairs rooms, and so they huddled for as long as possible in the kitchen.

The stranded guests included a middle-aged couple from "across the channel" in town for the Armistice; a trio of ragged backpackers taking shelter from the storm, and two German spinsters doing research on their relatives at the nearby German WWII cemetery. None of them wanted to be the first to venture upstairs to their cold, dark rooms until it was apparent that Madame D'Isgny and her husband were tired of entertaining them. They handed out extra blankets and led their guests upstairs in a flickering caravan to their rooms. Riley could hear the others laughing and chatting while she sat alone watching candle shadows chase each other across the wall.

CHAPTER 32

THE VISION

MADAME D'ISGNY LOOKED UP from the front desk with an exasperated sigh. Despite the fact that it was sunny outside, despite the fact that the long puddles in front of the hotel would soon evaporate, it could take a week to restore electricity to the towns along the coast. And phone service—two weeks. Where did the young American think she was? New York City? Being without electricity or the phone was hardly something to fret about. They'd lived through much worse during the War. Why not just relax? Young people are so, how is the word, energetique. Madame D'Isny did assure Riley that she'd been able to get through to Roger Saski at the hospital. Madame Saski had a concussion but would survive.

Relax? Riley thought. How? She and Simone had almost been killed and now she was stranded in a small fishing village. Relax? The very thought of relaxing made her even more nervous.

The backpackers, however, were relaxed. Staying at the hotel (even without electricity) had been a luxury for them. Soon the three—Michel, Jean Luis and Pierre—would resume their trek, sleeping in the open, drinking coffee from a tin can, eating donated bread and cheese while walking fifteen to twenty miles a day. They were on a pilgrimage to a holy shrine, Saint something or other, in the Pyrenees.

As they prepared to leave, Michel had a vision. It was God's will that the young American should join them on their pilgrimage.

Really?

Mais oui! God wants you to come with us. Yes, He created zees big storm so that we could meet. Yes, it was God's will.

Riley had to admit, they were the cutest God-guys she'd ever met. Michel and Jean Luis had dark tousled hair and soulful brown eyes; Pierre was a gangly, goofy blonde. She imagined the letter she would write to her uncle.

Dear Uncle Bob, I've decided to go on a pilgrimage to Saint Sebastian's tomb with Michel, Jean-Louis and Pierre, three really religious and cute Frenchmen. I don't know how I'll get home but Michel claims that it's God's will and so...

Riley chuckled. As amusing as it was to imagine her uncle's reaction to getting such a letter, basically the she hated to camp under the stars, especially if she had no idea where her next meal was coming from. So, she told them "no" and watched sadly as they left on their spiritual quest.

The German ladies were also relaxed. They noted matter-of-factly that Germany had more dependable phone and electrical service (of course!) but they were made of sturdy stuff. Casually they packed a lunch and left to find the graves of soldiers whose families had no idea what happened to them. Yes. There was misery on both sides, they reminded Riley. And innocence.

After all of the guests left on their various adventures, Riley had nothing to do but feel sorry for herself. Abandoned, forgotten, trapped. No money, no friends, in a small fishing village mopping up after a huge storm.

Before long Madame D'Isgny tired of watching the her mope about and gave her a job—peeling potatoes for the chowder they'd have for lunch—which is where, when he arrived on the scene, Roger Saski found Riley. He was low on sleep and drained of color. Simone would need to stay in the hospital for at least a week and so he was there to gather their things and move to a hotel closer to the hospital.

"What happened to the back window of my car?" he asked.

"Simone didn't tell you?"

"She has no memory of anything beyond our first night at the hotel."

"Really?"

"Yeah, the last few days are a complete blank."

"Well. The burgermeister followed us to the hotel."

"You're kidding?"

"No, I'm not. Before the storm he was in our room, probably looking for Charlie's key chain. He probably doesn't know that Lou has it! And then, he must've followed us up the hill. We were on the way to get you. Simone was worried you'd have a heart attack and die because you'd be so worried about her. She thought we could outrun the storm but it came onshore way too fast."

"She's been like a mother hen since my close call. So he

followed you and…what happened?"

"He tried to ram us off the cliff. You see the car stalled, and we were just like sitting ducks."

"And the back window?"

"Your gun—I just kept firing it at him."

"Well, I'll be damned. Did you kill the damn Nazi?"

"No, he's in the hospital too, but I don't think it was because of me. I probably just scared him away and then his car slid into the side of a building—at least that's what the stupid gardien de la paix thinks. Somehow I managed to get the car to start and drove us back to the hotel."

Roger lit a cigarette. "Son of a bitch. I'd better contact Lou. I guess he didn't…oh well. He'll take care of it." Then he went to find Madame D'Isgny and convince her to let him use the sacred radio. After he left Riley ran upstairs to grab her things thinking that naturally, Roger would take her along with him.

Outside the mists were rising over the Cotentin Peninsula. Thousands of sea gulls descended on overturned trash cans, angrily squawking at each other as they fought for the best treats. The bay shimmered in the sun, innocently, as though the previous day had never happened.

When Roger finally made it up to their suite of rooms he found Riley staring out the window, her body completely drained of the adrenalin that had kept her a awake for most of the night. "Boy, that car's a mess," he said, "I'll be lucky to get it to Bayeux."

"I can't wait to get out of here. Simone says they make fantastic chocolate crepes in Bayeux. I can't wait to try them."

"Oh, you're not going with me."

"What?"

"Didn't your uncle call?"

"No. We have no phone service."

"Oh, that's right. I was supposed to tell you," he said. "The last twenty-four hours have been so crazy, I don't know whether I'm a-coming or a-going, as my granny used to say. The thing is, someone is coming to pick you up; I believe you know the young man. He's one of Lou's young Turks—don't recall his name."

"Gil?"

"Yes, that's it—Gil. Your uncle's still in Paris so Gil's going to drive you there. Mighty nice of him, I thought," Roger said with a wink. "This place isn't exactly on the route to Paris from Amsterdam."

Riley could feel her cheeks burning and her heart quickening. "Are you sure I shouldn't come with you and then take a train to Paris."

"Oh no, he's on his way."

CHAPTER 33

SPLIT ENDS

GIL WAS COMING. At first the thought filled Riley with dread. Then giddiness. She began to fret about where she should be when he arrived. Walking barefoot on the beach, her long hair blowing in the breeze as she chatted amicably with the villagers, or curled up on a sofa in one of the hotel's parlors, writing letters home, the very picture of a Victorian heroine. Should she act happy to see him or cavalier? Should she tell him about the Burgermeister or would he think she was overreacting to a simple car accident on a stormy night as the gardien suggested?

Then it dawned on her. Gil already knew everything. Probably via the same network through which Lou Raferman always seemed to know everything—even with phone lines down, and no power. Yes, that was it. Lou had ordered him to retrieve her: *Go get that idiot before she really shoots someone.* Yes that was it. Gil was only coming because it was an order and not because he cared enough to go out of his way for her. It was an assignment, just like showing her Lou's apartment or picking her up from the train had been. Only part of his job.

What a fool she'd been. What a fool to think for a minute that he was interested in her. Thank goodness she'd come to her senses in time. Oh sure, he'd act pleasant because he was a gentleman, but secretly he would be counting the hours before he could get rid of her. The only way to save face, she decided, was to pretend she didn't care what he thought. He was, after all, just like all other expats who'd assumed the veneer of decadent sophistication, losing what it meant to be an American, to have hope, to have dreams, to aspire. Cynical was the word for those poor souls and cynical she would never be.

For the next few hours Riley had to live with herself in this state, fighting her poor heart with 100 percent surety of ungodly embarrassment should she lose control, practicing what she would say and how she would act, knowing full well that when he arrive, she would forget everything and stammer like a blubbering idiot.

Eventually, the dress rehearsal for the *event* grew tiresome. She took the book she'd stolen from her uncle's bookcase out of her backpack and sat at the Saskis' special table in a corner window of the restaurant trying to understand why this book so captivated her uncle. His edition (edited by Willard Thorp of Princeton, no less) contained over a hundred chapters babbling on about harpoons and even sailor's knots, for crying out loud. On the inside back cover was a chart contrasting different literary opinions about meaning and symbolism. Riley wondered what the author, Herman Melville, would have thought if he could see what an industry his opus had generated. If he had a vision while cataloguing spears and whalebones that every word would be analyzed and argued over for centuries.

Eventually her mind drifted from Melville to her split ends. Specifically the multi-pronged split ends she'd managed to accumulate over the past few years. She held them up to the light, fascinated by the destruction and then, using her front teeth as scissors, bit them off. Let Ahab go in search of some whale, she thought I have split ends to track down and harpoon.

*　*　*

"You know they do have scissors in France." Gil said after sneaking up upon her.

"I know that!"

"Don't get upset. I'm only teasing."

To her horror, he was not alone. Her name was Vivienne and she was a beautiful Asian woman, fluent in five languages and skinny as a fashion model. He claimed she was a friend who needed a ride to the American Embassy in Paris where she worked. Of course, Riley thought, the American Embassy. Where else would a drop-dead gorgeous, glamorous, and sophisticated woman work? A woman who probably savored lapin au jus and escargot, who sipped wine and didn't guzzle, who got manicures and pedicures and wore high heels. Someone who probably didn't have, and had never even heard of, split ends.

"You can sit in the front," Vivienne offered, as they prepared to leave.

"No, I want to ride in the back."

"Really. I don't mind."

"No, no. I'll ride in back"

"Ladies, please don't fight over who *has* to ride in front with me," Gil said. "It hurts my feelings."

He didn't look like his feelings were hurt. He looked like he was poking fun of both of them.

"I just didn't sleep well last night. I was hoping to get some shut eye on our way to Paris." Riley explained. This excuse worked.

"Of course," Vivienne said. "After what you've been through."

"What do you mean?"

"Oh, I heard you had an accident and that the lady you were with is in the hospital. That must have been horrible."

"If you don't mind, I don't really want to talk about it." Perfect Miss Vivienne already knows everything, she thought as she climbed into the backseat of Gil's car. On their long drive down the coast, he'd probably entertained her with Riley stories: How she'd mistaken a bidet for a toilet. How she'd run away from the Swiss Police because of some imaginary threat to her life. How she'd been kidnapped on the Metro only to reappear completely unharmed. And now this accident in a rainstorm involving, of all things, an evil Burgermeister.

They probably can't wait to drop me at my uncle's hotel so that they can dine on escargot and lapin au jus and laugh at how silly I've been, she thought. The silly, silly American girl. And she dwelt on that thought and no other for hours as they negotiated road closures and detours. For hours as she pretended to sleep but heard every bit of sophisticated banter between Gil and the Perfect Vivienne.

CHAPTER 34

A COUPLE OF LOSERS

"SO LET ME GET THIS STRAIGHT. This fellow goes out of his way to drive to the coast to pick you up on possibly *the worst day* to drive around rural France and you won't even have dinner with him. Supposedly because you don't care about him and you think he's in love with some other woman. And then you cry your eyes out all night long."

"I wasn't crying about Gil. I miss my boyfriend. Besides, Gil only came to get me because Lou Raferman made him."

Riley and her uncle were on the platform waiting for the one train headed to Germany that day. The death of Charles DeGaulle had crippled the country. All businesses were closed or on reduced hours and it was impossible to get through on any phone line. "Really? How do you know that? Did he tell you?"

"No, but it doesn't matter. Didn't *you* tell me to stay away from him."

"I did? I must have had a few. I happen to know he volunteered to come pick you up."

His own mission to Paris had been a failure. His wife did not want to be saved. "Especially by the *heartless, spineless, cheating bastard* who rejected her. I even tried of-

187

fering Stephano money to disappear. But apparently it wasn't money enough to dissuade him from the American dream. Your poor aunt."

"Oh my God. You didn't try to bribe him in front Auntie Sue, did you?"

"What kind of a schlep do you think I am?"

Riley didn't dare answer.

"Listen, your auntie is convinced that she's met her soul mate and that *he* can't live without her when in reality that man would marry a goat if that's what it took to get to the US. Everyone can see it but her. You and I are some pair, aren't we?" he said as their train pulled into the station. "You've got a good guy, legitimately interested, but you turn and run. And I took a small-town girl far from home, introduced her to, well, more than she was equipped to handle and now she's about to throw her life away. Yup, we're quite a pair."

"Maybe she'll—"

"Come to her senses? You've never been in love have you?"

"Sure. I love my boyfriend."

"The one you left behind to come to Europe for... How many months has it been now? Ha!"

CHAPTER 35

THE BIG GAME HUNTER

A WEEK LATER the Saskis made a surprise visit to Happy Hour, Simone in a neck brace that made her stand even stiffer than she had before. She still had no memory of the storm. No memory of the burgermeister ramming her car, no memory of that entire day. The head injury had affected her in other ways too; she giggled less at the raunchy jokes told on barstools, instead, clinging to Roger, her fingers trembling as she lit those endless cigarettes. At first Riley thought her uncle would be devastated, that he would start drinking more than usual, miss work, toss aside his grooming habits but the opposite was true. The reason was Lou Raferman's perpetually cheerful clerk-typist, Molly. She was, as the saying goes, a good-time gal to whom every day was a party.

And the burgermeister? He returned to Worms at about the same time as the Saskis but his stay was very brief. Within a week the local paper announced that he'd resigned. According to the story, a recent, almost fatal accident had convinced him life was too short to delay a long-cherished childhood dream, which in his case were to become a big-game hunter. There was even a picture of the him, dressed in safari gear, leaning against a long-barreled rifle. It was, of course, clipped and passed around the officers' club for everyone's amusement. *What a joke! A big game hunter!*

They all laughed as if yesterday's villains could put on clown's suits and dance across the stage and all would be forgiven. As if it was possible to just forget the past and move on. But Riley couldn't forget the horror of that stormy night in Normandy. How dark the skies suddenly became; how the rain hit the roof of the car like machine gun fire; how the car had spun out of control. And then, when they were helpless, when in front of them was the cliff and far below the cliff, the sea crashing against the rocks, the Burgermeister rolled by them with a look she knew she'd never forget.

"Why did Lou Raferman want that film so much if he wasn't planning to do something?"

"He doesn't like messy endings."

"Yeah but …"

"Drop it kiddo. Look at it this way: perhaps the Burgermeister will get eaten by a lion."

"Is Lou planning to have him eaten by a lion."

"Sure kid, if it makes you feel any better. Lou Raferman has arranged for the Burgermeister to be eaten by a lion."

* * *

A grey curtain had been stretched over the German. skies. A grey curtain that rarely opened. Snow, when it fell, froze into slush. Riley took a couple of short trips (London and Amsterdam) with the sister-in-law of one of her uncle's colleagues, a woman considerably older but a woman who had money and was in need of a companion, a companion with a car and an International Driver's license. On the way home from one of those trips (London) the VW had broken down and they'd had to wait for repairs. As a result Riley had missed another dependent's flight home. It also meant she'd missed signing up for the spring semester. She could miss one semester but missing two in a row meant she'd have to jump through all kinds of hoops to reenter her program.

"I still want to go home," she told her uncle.

"But you'll have to get a low paying job until next fall. Why don't you get that low paying job here instead—at least you'll get the experience of really living in Europe?"

"But—"

"I'll sign you up for the army typing test. It's so easy that any moron can pass it. Thirty-five words a minute; that's all you need to be able to type. Who can't type that fast? And then you can work for the army during the week and finish your travels on the weekends."

Riley thought about it. He was right. If she went home now, she'd have nothing to do until the fall. Except work at some crappy job. "I did take typing my freshman year of high school."

"Good. Then I'll sign you up."

★ ★ ★

On the morning of the test (a Saturday in mid December), the Rhine River valley was as frigid as a meat locker. As a result Riley arrived at the compound in Worms a human popsicle. And, because the road had been cov-

191

ered in ice, she was also five minutes late. With no time to thaw, she was sat in front of a manual typewriter with a text to retype that contained multiple capitalizations, numbers and quotation marks—all massive roadblocks to someone unaccustomed to typing daily. Ready. Set. Go.

For the ascribed three minutes she pounded on the stiff keys, her fingers slipping repeatedly between the J and F. Then the buzzer rang and the end product was revealed.

Fail. Too few words; too many typos.

She was given another chance.

Same result. Unfortunately she wasn't the only person taking the test. The other was a serious-looking young man. He passed the test on the first try but for some reason stayed to watch Riley fail for a second and third time.

"No one has ever failed the army typing test three times," the officer in charge told her bluntly. "You'll have to wait a couple of weeks to try again."

That was the last straw. "I'm going home," she informed her uncle, as they listened to canned Christmas music in the half empty officers' club.

"Failed the army typing test? Sheesh, Niecey, how can I show my face in the office again?"

"My fingers were frozen. The heater in the Volkswagen is a joke!"

"They must have warmed up by your *third* attempt!"

"I just want to go home."

"I bet I could get Molly to tutor you. She must type ninety words a minutes with no errors. Let's invite her over for dinner."

"I know what you're after."

"Hey, *she* can type!"

"I'm just not a typist. And besides, she wouldn't be coming over to help me; she'd be after you!"

He laughed. "Aren't all women? I've got them lined up down the street. All wanting a bit of this!" He pinched the roll over his belt and shook it. Many of the happy hour regulars had returned stateside to visit with their families for the holiday season. For those stuck in Germany, the manager of the club tried to cheer up the place with plastic garlands and poinsettia plants. Then he'd invited a wide variety of vendors from Scotland, Turkey, and Morocco (to name just a few) to hawk their wares from long folding tables set up in the dining room.

"No, Uncle Bob, I want to go. I've been such a failure at everything."

"How about old Gilberto? I heard he's coming back in a few weeks. You weren't too rough on him in Paris, were you?"

"I screwed that up too—if there was anything to screw up to begin with. Besides I haven't heard from him since Paris."

"Oh, I thought you heard. He had to fly back to the states. His grandmother passed away."

"Oh, God." Riley hadn't even considered that Gil might have a family. A mother, a father, siblings, grandparents, uncles and aunts—cousins. "This is going to be a terrible Christmas for him."

"You don't say. Listen, there are other things we can get you into—like the American University down in Heidelberg. Lou has contacts—he could get you in."

"Lou thinks I'm a complete moron."

"That was before he knew you could shot a gun."

"What?"

"Kidding, just kidding. Someone always need a driver, kiddo, and you do seem able to find your way around. That little escapey pooh from Switzerland on backroads through France took some gumption. It impressed Lou who knows that area well. Speaking of which, the only other moron to flunk the Army Typing Test three times was Lou Raferman. He think flunking that test is sign of genius."

The American University did had a reputation for accepting the majority of the army dependents who applied but what if some reason they rejected her? No, she said, better to hurry on home with at least some shred of dignity. Besides, she'd announced to her family and friends that she was coming home. The deal was done.

CHAPTER 36

OPA GETS FRISKY

"CHRIST. DID YOU READ THIS CRAP?"

Uncle Bob was referring to a letter that had been been passed to him at the bar by the blonde named Annie. The Happy Hour crowd had dwindled to half its usual size.

"She just wants to come by and get a few things." Annie said. Earlier that day she'd put her own four children on a dependent's flight to the States to spend Christmas with her parents..

"Niecey, we better head for home and hide all the valuables."

"Bob—"

"Tell her she can come by when I'm at work but she'd better not—"

"She won't."

"Promise? Hey, now that the kids are gone, you and Dougie can really kick up your heels."

Annie looked over at her husband who was deep into his third Martini. "Yeah," she said.

* * *

The next morning, the snow, which never melted because the sun never came out, covered everything. But it wasn't fluffy snow; it was like Styrofoam. However, that did not deter Riley's aunt in the least as she hauled load after load out of the house in Gunthersblum. She was in love. She'd finally met a man who treated her like a goddess; something she'd never known before ("certainly not with your uncle!"). He showered her with wild flowers he'd plucked from the fields and kissed her all over ("and I mean *all over—even my C-section scars!"*) Not to mention the sex! The multiple orgasms! Her giggles, as she described their sexual romps in mortifying detail, had a hypnotic effect on the old man who lived across the street. He watched the two women from the window as they loaded up the car and then, unable to control himself, he'd trotted out to join them, throwing his arms around the aunt and lifting her up in the air.

"Opa, shame!" she giggled. "Naughty!"

The more she scolded him the more excited he became. He smacked his lips. "Schatzie! Kuss mich, kuss mich," he cried as he chased her around the car trying to squeeze her ample derriere. Finally, his wife heard the commotion and ran out shouting threats (something to do with disposing of his manhood). He scowled and gave his Schatzie last, juicy kiss before following his wife back to their house.

For some reason Riley thought she could succeed where her uncle had failed. That she could make her aunt realize that the great love of her life might be using her to get to America. But she would do it gently. Woman to woman.

"Auntie Sue, are you sure this guy isn't using you?"

It was a huge mistake. Any suggestion for caution fell on ears treated to words of love whispered so fervently that she expected to hear them every moment of every day, year after year, for the rest of her life. This was the happy path her life now took, and if Riley didn't believe her, then she should visit them in Paris to bear witness to the *truth*.

"I know what," she said. "I'll show you how much he adores me. You can come for Christmas! You'll love it! The Champs-Élysées all lit up. So romantic. So beautiful! You don't want to stay here with Bob! He'll probably drag you to one of the general's holiday parties!"

"Oh, I don't think so, but thanks."

"Think about it!"

"Are you sure I wouldn't be in the way?"

"Oh no. We'll have a good time."

Ah, Riley's dilemma. On the one hand, Christmas in Paris. On the other, Christmas at her uncle's house, writing bullshit letters home.

"But I can't leave Uncle Bob alone at Christmas."

"Bob, alone?" She laughed. "Are you kidding? Annie says he was planning to leave *you* alone and take off with Lou's newest secretary!"

Riley started to object "He wouldn't do that..." but then seeing the look on her aunt's face , sighed: "Oh yeah he probably would." And she was right. Her uncle had already packed his bags and bought tickets for a ski adventure in Austria. He didn't ski but then, neither did Molly.

CHAPTER 37

CHRISTMAS IN PARIS

AUNTIE AND HER LOVER were temporarily staying in one of the thousands of apartments located in Ivry, a working class borough somewhere south of central Paris. The apartment belonged to Lover Boy's uncle who was on vacation. When he returned, they would have to find another place to live but by then Auntie was certain Lou Raferman could pull enough strings that they could fly directly back to the United States to start their wonderful life together, preferably in Florida! Auntie spoke rapidly and breathlessly and she drove like she spoke.

They arrived in late evening, Auntie admitting with a giggle that they hadn't been in *that* particular apartment for *that* long. But she was *pretty sure* they were in the right neighborhood. No, amend that. She was sure that it was *probably* the right neighborhood and *so let's park the car in this alleyway and find the place. I'll know it when I see it!*

Such assurances weren't reassuring to Riley. In the falling snow all the buildings looked the same. I wonder when they'll realize we're probably dead, she thought as she dragged one of her aunt's massive suitcases block after block through the slushy snow. The shops and restaurants had closed for the night and there were no people on the streets. How long will it take until someone realizes we got lost wandering the streets trying to figure out which of the hundreds of plain brick apartment buildings lover boy's uncle lived in, until, exhausted and half-frozen, we'd slumped into a snowbank and died. Days? Weeks? Until the snow thawed?

"Maybe we should try and call him," Riley suggested when they stumbled upon a pay phone booth.

"Oh no! There it is! Above that market!" Auntie giggled. "See, love will always find a way!"

"Are you sure?" Save for a few lights on the upper floors, the building she pointed to was dark and unwelcoming.

"Oh yeah!"

She charged across the street and rattled about at the front door until it opened. "See, the key works!"

The apartment Lover Boy and Auntie were staying in only had three rooms: a bedroom, a small kitchen and a living room which also doubled as a dining room. There was no bathroom. All of the residents of the fourth floor shared a communal bathroom down the hall, but, Auntie explained with another giggle, "There is a bucket in the coat closet near the front door for emergencies."

"You've got to be kidding."

"You have to learn to live like a European. Don't worry. Most of the people on this floor are from Greece and they've all gone back home for the holidays."

Lover Boy deigned to stick his head out from the bedroom for a brief introduction. But not much more. After a week's absence, Auntie couldn't wait to drag him back to the bed where he would have to pay dearly for her efforts to get him to the promised land. "You can sleep on the sofa near the window, she said handing Riley a blanket and pillow. "Just don't disturb Lemon and Lime!"

"Lemon and Lime?"

"The parakeets."

What a day, Riley thought as she watched snow fall on the umbrellas in the open air market below. What a day. Listening to her aunt go on and on about her wonderful lover only to find out he was a scrawny, sullen, creepy guy with an unhealthy complexion. What would her grandmother say if she knew that her youngest son, her baby, had a mistress and that his wife had left him for a man half her age? *Lord have mercy. Lord have mercy. What a scandal. How can I show my face in town anymore?* Granny lived in such a different world. A world that seemed so far away.

The snow fell quietly on the umbrellas in the square below and on rooftops stretching to the horizon. Falling endlessly. Falling so quietly. For a time the birds hanging in their cage above her head made little chirping sounds and then they and Riley drifted off on a snowflake.

* * *

Lemon and Lime awoke in a dither. The sun has risen over the sleepy white world and their cage was still covered! "Nasty little birdies," Riley told the two as she uncovered their cage. She'd wanted to sleep a little bit longer but their dithering caused bird seed to rain down upon her head and it hurt. "Although, if I had to live in a birdcage in a tiny apartment, I'd put up a fuss." She said, shaking bird crap from her hair and clothes as she rose.

"Morning Riley! I've been up since five making cherry pies! Come help me!" Her aunt called from the kitchen. "I've got to make at least a dozen!"

Well, Riley thought, at least I know what I'll be doing today.

As Lover Boy slept, the two women worked. Rolling out the dough. Preparing the filling. Assembling the pies and then very carefully watching as they baked in a tiny oven with no temperature gauge. By evening, the dining room table was covered with pies. Each more perfect than the one before. Lover Boy poked his head out of the bedroom around five asking for a coffee. That evening he had a job as a bartender, Auntie explained. That's what he'd done in Greece and he was a *wonderful* bartender and all the resorts wanted him to work for them. Although he wanted to be a chef and so when they moved to the US, that's what he'd do!

By the end of the day all that pie making in a cramped and overheated apartment had taken the stuffing out of Riley. But her aunt had other ideas.

"Get freshened up young lady, we're going down to the Champs-Élysées. You cannot miss the light show! You just can't!"

And so they climbed aboard a packed bus and rode to the center of Paris. Just Riley and her aunt, buying roasted chestnuts from one of the many street vendors and envying the many lovers strolling down boulevards lined with enchanted trees.

* * *

The Christmas onslaught began in early afternoon and Auntie was ready. Each guest arrived bearing a something. A casserole of some sort or another, a loaf of homemade bread or rolls, a bottle of wine or jug of hard cider and left with a cherry pie. Most of them lived in the building and had known Lover Boy since he was a child and visited his uncle on holidays. They ate and ate and ate taking only an occasional break so the men could check on the results of the daylong horse races while the women gossiped and cleaned dishes in the kitchen.

By late afternoon Riley was ready to curl up under Lemon and Lime and call it a day. No more food could possibly enter her body. But then the final guests arrived with a roast goose and they sat down at the table.

* * *

The next day, Riley caught the train back to Germany, leaving her aunt happily peeing in a chamber pot for love everlasting. Cheerfully planning a future that would include a loving and faithful husband, a twinkle in her soft brown eyes, dimpled cheeks pink with joy.

Simone met her at the train station. "Your uncle is still in Austria but you are welcome to stay with us until he returns."

"Does he know that I'm leaving on New Years Day?".

"Most definitely, but he is with Molly, you see."

"How do you feel about that?"

"Why should I not be happy for him? I hope you are hungry. I have made couscous. And then tomorrow we shop for the galette des roi."

"A cake?"

"Mais oui but not just a *cake*. A galette only made once a year. You will not want to miss this!"

Oh goody. More food, Riley thought. Her stomach still ached from the Christmas orgy of food.

CHAPTER 38

GALETTE DES ROI

NOTHING IN THE BASE COMMISSARY was good enough for Simone's Galette des Roi and so the next day they went on a crusade. A crusade to find only the freshest and best ingredients. A crusade which would lead them across the border to the area of France where she had grown up, the Alsace. First, they stopped at a hole in the wall that sold only spices, thousands of spices all stored in glass canisters lining the aged oak shelves. Their quest: vanilla from Madagascar and only Madagascar, *naturellement*. Next, they drove to the other side of town for nuts. almonds from Turkey and only Turkey, *naturellement*. By then it was time for lunch. A leisurely lunch at a cafe on the river running through the town of Nancy.

Their day ended with a visit to a small farm on the outskirts of town "Are we going to milk the cows and make our own butter?"

Simone smiled. "No, you smarty pants. But we scoop the butter out of the vat and package it ourselves! It is the only way!"

* * *

Day Two they cracked and blanched Turkish almonds.

Pounds and pounds of Turkish almonds which Roger then ground into paste using a pestle and mortar. That was the one and only task that Simone trusted him to do; the rest she would do alone while Riley kept her company.

"I can help."

"I make these galettes every year for so many year now that it is like meditation. I like to have the company but the tasks I must do myself. Tu comprends? I think of the year and all the sorrows and also the happinesses. In France we have these galettes on the Epiphany mais we go to Lou Raferman big fete on New Years Eve and he insist on galette des roi. You come to the party with us, non?"

The last time, indeed the only time she'd been to Lou's penthouse apartment, Gil had been there. They'd stood on the balcony and listened to the music coming from the outdoor restaurants along the river. "You should stay," he'd told her. "Experience Europe." And silly her, she'd thought he wanted her to stay.

"I think I'll probably be too busy packing."

"We shall see." Simone said with a wink. "I think we take you to officer's club at least. To say adieu to your friends."

"But—"

"There is no but!"

* * *

Day Three all the ingredients for the galettes were ready for the assemblage, an activity for which Simone welcomed the help. Each galette had to have a *fève*, she explained, buried within the pastry layers—a miniature porcelain Jesus or Mother Mary. Traditionally the person who got the slice with the fève was crowned king and had to wear a paper crown for the rest of the Epiphany. But she'd promised Lou seven galettes each containing a *fève*. "Such silliness. He's bought seven crowns."

"What if someone swallows the baby Jesus?" Riley asked.

Roger chuckled, "Some bakeries put a kidney bean in the filling for that very reason. They don't want anyone choking on the baby Jesus and then complaining."

"A bean! Why cannot people just eat slowly?" No bean would ever take the place of a *fève* in Simone's galettes!

Once they were done, and all ten galettes sat on the side table in the Saski's dining room smelling divine and baked to the perfect golden tone, Simone opened a bottle of champagne and they toasted their accomplishment. "So are you going to teach your mother to make the Galette des Roi?"

"Oh, I don't think so. There aren't any speciality shops in Reno so I'd have to use whatever I could find in the supermarket. Besides my mother doesn't bake. I imagine these are the last Galette des Roi I'll be making."

Simone gave her a hug. "This cannot be. You cannot have these galette only once in your lifetime."

In two days I'll be back in Reno Nevada, Riley thought, and Simone's kitchen will be a distant memory. A distant memory full of warmth and determination, of traditions lasting for generations, even through wars and tremendous suffering. Americans were so untested. In many ways, it frightened her. Europeans had learned to adjust their expectations but could Americans? She thought of the last time she'd talked to her boyfriend. Campus issues weighed heavily in his mind. She'd listened to him go on and on about budget meetings and other things which seemed so trivial. *Oh, you have to stay in Europe another month. No problem. We have student elections and the judges have their quarterly meeting and so I'll be busy anyway.* She wondered whether her return was even something he looked forward to. Still, what choice did she have? Her prospects in Europe were slim.

CHAPTER 39

COME SING THIS SONG OF JOY

EVERY PASSENGER on the dependent flight home held either a wailing toddler or screeching infant on their lap. The no-frills flight would stop first in Washington DC and then continue on to LA, taking twenty-one hours in total. *Twenty one hours in a tin can filled mostly with women and children, expecting only crackers and water from the barebones crew, what am I doing*, Riley asked herself. The baby on her lap howled. He had wet diapers and mucus running from his nose into his mouth. Next to them, his mother wept as a restless toddler wiggled on her lap.

At first the promised on-time departure seemed like extreme folly on the part of the pilot. The worst fog in thirty years had descended on southern Germany, grounding most flights and even disrupting some rail travel. But, after some debate with the tower, the pilot, a Navy ace rumored to have flown dozens of combat missions in Vietnam, announced they were taking off. There was a collective gasp and then the plane began rolling down the tarmac, its engines straining for take off.

Riley looked out the window but all she could see was fog as thick as cement. *What am I doing*, she asked herself again as she remembered that last kiss. *What am*

I doing?

She had not slept the night before, nor had she'd even seen a bed. She'd arrived in Gunthersblum two hours before flight time to find her duffel bag packed and on the backseat of the VW and her uncle stewing over a cup of coffee in the kitchen.

"It looked pretty passionate back there. Are you sure you know what you're doing?" Uncle Bob asked as they drove through fog so thick they couldn't tell if they were on the road or not.

"Oh, you mean that kiss? Gil will forget me as soon as Elke gets her claws into him."

"Whatever you say, kid. Hey, stick your head out and make sure we're still on the road. I think we're on the shoulder. Hell, we might even be in a field."

"It's zero degrees out there! Say, why aren't I driving?"

"Hell, you think the police are going to be up at the crack of dawn on New Year's Day in this mess? Ha! Boy oh boy, you sure did cut it close. Did I mention you're flying standby? "

She felt like telling her uncle that it was all his fault for running into Gil and bringing him back to the officer's club where she'd been plied with too many farewell drinks to think straight. He should have taken her home to pack instead of disappearing in the crowd with Molly. She'd been ready to leave Europe and never look back. Ready to patch up things with a boyfriend who'd grown increasingly distant. Ready to take some crappy job until she could get back into school. Ready to go back to the basement apartment she shared with a girl from Winnemucca. All ready.

And there stood Gil, smiling as if he'd always been with her. A few breathless moments later someone in the crowd noticed the time. 11:30. If they ran they could catch the last train to Heidelberg. And run they did. Along the river in the lightly falling snow, passing restaurant barges all decorated for the season and blasting the same song: *Freude, schöner Götterfunken Tochter aus Elysium, Wir betreten feuertrunken.* Giddily they made up their own lyrics: *Weiner Schnitzel, Bitte Danke, Guten Tagen, Wiedersehen,* Laughing in that snow globe world as if the night would never end.

They'd reached the station just as the train to Heidelberg was departing. As soon as the conductor blew his final whistle, they joined the stampede of happy revelers clamoring onboard the already moving train. Gil grabbed Riley's arm and pulled her through the crowds. Car after car until they found empty seats and snuggled together by the window. If the world ends tonight, Riley thought, I'm right where I want to be, listening to the clanking of the wheels and the laughter coming from the next car.

But it hadn't taken long for Elke and Sam from Colorado to track them down and claim the empty seats across from them.

"You are not a regular at the happy hour," Elke said to Gil. "Where are you hiding?"

"I'm based in Worms, but I travel a lot," He turned to Riley. "I did make it back in time for Christmas but I couldn't find you."

"I was in Paris with my aunt."

"How was it?"

"Interesting. I don't think I've ever eaten so much —"

"So Gil," Elke butted in. "You work for Raferman?"

"Say, what is it that you do, Elke? That's your name, isn't it?"

"Do? What do you mean, do?"

"Gil means are you employed? Do you work for someone or just hang out at the officers' club."

"You are drunk!" she snarled at her date.

"Yes I am. Delightfully drunk."

"German men do not get drunk like this."

"Oh yeah? Well if they're so wonderful why do you want to leave Germany?"

"I have career."

"Bull," Sam muttered before passing out on Elke's lap.

"Ach! He drools like a dog on my skirt! What is wrong this man?" she snarled, shaking him off and rising to her feet.

"He did a tour in Nam. So cut him some slack."

"He does not have to act like animal." She left Sam passed out on the seat and proceeded to push in next to Gil. "No, I cannot be with a man who is like dog. What is your GS, Geel?"

"What's a GS?" Riley asked, as he leaned closer to her.

"Government service ranking. It'll tell her how much money I make and what my pension will look like," he said sarcastically. Elke began to object but he cut her off. "Look! There's the castle."

"Wow. It's so big."

"Those are the ruins of the original castle. War and Mother Nature have taken their toll. It will probably never be rebuilt."

"Why?"

"Well it was hit by lightening twice and you know what happens to those who tempt fate a third time."

Elke opened her mouth to say something but the cheers of the passengers as the train doors opened drowned her out. "Frohes Neues Jahr!! The noise also rousted Sam who sat up and looked around confused. The same woman who'd previously hung all over him, now discarded him like a dirty tissue. He made several awkward attempts to hold Elke's hand as they exited the train. Each time she brushed him away. Riley felt like screaming "run for your life" to both men, but Gil, who always seemed to know what she was thinking, whispered, "Just stay cool. It will all work out okay," then he dropped back to steady Sam while she took Elke's arm.

Along the route, street vendors worked feverishly to keep up with orders for beer and kazoos from the river of revelers. In that moment they were not German or French or Italian or even American. They were free from the past, free from their separate islands of prejudice as they sang "Come sing this song of joy" and marched uphill to storm the storybook castle.

They'd just managed to reach the middle of town when the fireworks began. At first they fizzled in the falling snow or created mini starbursts in the clouds. But then they began to gain in intensity until the sky was filled with iridescent glitter, glitter that mingled with the snowflakes falling to the ground around them. The conclusion was a silver and gold explosion over the medieval castle that exposed the ghosts of the past inhabitants, who, decked out in their armor and jewels, stood on the battlements for a glimpse of the living.

After the fireworks, the magic spell broke as people hustled toward the train station, hustled toward their cars, their motorcycles or anything that would get them out of the increasing cold. Gil suggested they wait out the mass exodus in a crowded bar.

"I know why you never come to the officers' club," Riley whispered to Gil, as Elke continued to sulk in the seat across from them.

"It's like drinking at a zoo. One false step will land you in the tiger's cage."

Riley closed her eyes and the next thing she knew, Gil was loading her into the backseat of a taxi alongside Elke and Sam. "I must have fallen asleep."

"Trust me … you didn't miss anything good. The cabby is Armenian and doesn't speak English so I've got to ride in front and help him navigate through this fog."

Elke cracked the window and lit up a cigarette.

"Do you have to smoke in the car?" Sam asked. She glared at him but threw the butt out into the dense fog along the river.

"Do you know what time it is?" Riley asked.

"Haven't a clue. It's New Years Eve!" Sam said. "Whoops, amend that. It must be New Years Day! Are you really leaving us? You can't really be leaving us!"

It was six a.m.

CHAPTER 40

LA HEAT WAVE

HER BOYFRIEND hadn't recognized her at first. He'd scanned the incoming crowds looking right past her. Her eyes were red and swollen, her long hair matted with baby spit-up, her clothes wrinkled and drenched in baby pee. Worse yet, she was dressed for snow in the middle of a midwinter LA heat wave. "What happened to you?" he asked as he suffered through a hug and quick kiss.

"I just spent twenty one hours with a crying baby on my lap, plus I haven't gotten any sleep in two days."

"Your uncle sounds like a real jerk! It was supposed to be a graduation present not a—"

"No, no. He's not so bad. It was me. I just..." She paused. At first she had seen her uncle as the shining example of the Ugly American but he wasn't. He was just trying to survive in a cynical postwar world where love was not the answer, at least not on its own, where the true-blue American values of fidelity and justice for all were impractical to nations torn by centuries of war. "You know, because of me all the villagers call him Oncle Boob! Can you imagine? Oncle Boob. Poor guy."

He didn't laugh. "Your last letters were just so strange."

Riley couldn't remember what she'd written. "Really?"

"Yeah and now…you're just so different."

He treated her as one would a soiled diaper, held between the thumb and first finger as they walked out to his car, two strangers in the middle of a day that felt like night to her. That *was* night to her.

"I'm going to be real busy this next semester, with student council and my job with the judge, I don't think I'll have much time to spend with you. What are you going to do now that you've missed sign up for school?" He asked.

"Practice my typing!" was her response.

www.ingramcontent.com/pod-product-compliance
Lightning Source LLC
Chambersburg PA
CBHW020410210626
46816CB00006BB/2209